PRECARIOUS

THE LIVING WORLD
BOOK TWO

PRECARIOUS

THE LIVING WORLD
BOOK TWO

Patricia Vestal

Sea of Mountains Press
North Carolina, USA

Precarious: The Living World Book Two by Patricia Vestal

ISBN: 978-1-7375849-2-6

Published by Sea of Mountains Press, North Carolina, USA
www.seaofmountainspress.com

For permissions contact:
Email: author@seaofmountainspress.com

Cover and book design by: Michelle Triggs Owen, www.ProjectDesignInc.com

Cover image credit: NASA, ESA, N. Smith (University of California, Berkeley), and The Hubble Heritage Team (STScI/AURA)

DEDICATION

Dedicated to those who cherish all living things

PRECARIOUS

THE LIVING WORLD
BOOK TWO

PROLOGUE

The Realm shuddered and vibrated. It was a place that was not a true place, a universe held together by the collective beings that inhabited it, called Synons. They struggled to stay intact, reaching inward for strength and outward for connection. They had never known terror, although they had witnessed it countless times in the inhabitants of Earth. Now a visceral understanding of that biological reaction spread through them. Their purpose was to maintain and strengthen the link between The Living World that encompassed all of Creation and the living things on Earth, especially the dominant species, humans. That link needed constant reinforcement; it was fraying at an accelerated rate that threatened the very existence of the Realm.

The Realm was bathed in a pulsating kaleidoscope of colors, dominated by pastels, punctuated by shafts and orbs of deep primary hues. In an instant, the energy-mind-spirit that comprised the Synons unified in one undulating motion, a tranquil rhythm that linked the many as one, but their fragile union was assailed by waves of turbulence.

A collective wail reverberated through the Synons' connection to Earth. The Living Earth was in anguish and lashing out.

CHAPTER ONE

Panic ran rampant through the summer tourist centers of the Great Smoky Mountains National Park. The forest was ablaze. The roads in and out of Gatlinburg, Pigeon Forge, and Sevierville, Tennessee, were in gridlock. The National Forest Service's ground and air activity level was at peak as thousands battled the fire threatening a national treasure and the lives of thousands.

"Will the bears get burned up?" Five-year-old Emma Goodsen's eyes brimmed with tears, her pudgy fingers gripping her car seat.

Her parents looked at each other with concern just as her older brother, Liam, piped up. "Sure. Everything will burn to a crisp."

"Liam!" Nina Goodsen shot her "keep your mouth shut!" look at her twelve-year-old son.

"Well, it's true." Liam pouted. "An' I bet some stupid human started the fire anyway."

"Animals sense natural disasters and run away from them, son."

They had been sitting on U.S. 441 for what seemed like hours, vehicles lined up in front of and behind them on the curvy road. Luck had been with them. Their vacation had ended that morning as they packed up with a sad farewell to Gatlinburg and the beginning of what was planned to be a short, pleasant drive to Cherokee, North Carolina, which the kids, especially Liam, were anxious to visit and immerse themselves in Native American culture. The week had been warm with clear blue skies. This morning, to the west and northwest heavy smoke, quite unlike the low, bluish haze which prompted their name, hung over the Smoky Mountains. The air was thick with a charred odor and the Goodsens had hurried their departure. Nina kept track on her smart phone of what was happening while her husband fidgeted behind the wheel, foot on the brake more than the gas.

"Nina, check the GPS for alternate routes to Cherokee," Gary suggested. "If we come to a turn-off I want to know if it might take us in that direction, out of this traffic. The fire is behind us. As long as we can keep going east or southeast we should be okay."

Nina was already fiddling with the GPS and peering at the screen. "It doesn't look like there are any roads off here coming up. But it hasn't yet calculated alternate routes."

The fire had begun small, possibly the consequence of careless campers not fully extinguishing a fire. It had quickly been spotted, with firefighting efforts begun immediately. However, strong winds swept embers and flames swiftly through late summer vegetation that was dry and growing brittle from months of unusual drought, easy prey for the voracious flames. A catastrophic fire threatened to move toward heavily populated areas, all of which had ordered evacuations. The Goodsens felt like the proverbial sitting ducks, stuck in a traffic jam in an otherwise idyllic spot with a monstrous dragon threatening to breathe fire down on them. No turn-off appeared. No accessible alternate route. They sat, easing slightly forward at intervals.

Emma finally cried herself to sleep. Liam was engrossed in an electronic game. Nina was about to doze off. The sky erupted. Thunderous peals like a symphony of kettle drums announced jagged slashes of lightning that appeared to strike right next to them. Rain fell in torrents, blown by fierce winds. Chunks of hail popped against the car.

"Well, maybe this will help put out the fire," Nina said, recovering from the jolt of the sudden storm.

"Yeah, if the lightning doesn't start more fires," Liam mumbled.

Emma was awake and screaming again. Nina was trying to quiet her when a rumbling vibration shook the car. "What!" Gary yelled, jerking the wheel and slamming on the brakes.

Sounds of screeching tires and crunching metal resounded, as the low rumbling beneath them ceased. A crevice gaped just behind them; the road ahead of them was cracked and buckling. Vehicles in front of them were turned in all directions, some on their sides or tops, some crushed between others. People were running and shouting.

"Earthquake?" Nina was astounded.

"I think so," Gary agreed. "I didn't know they had them here, but they can happen anywhere."

Liam put down his window and stuck his head out, peering up at the sky. "Too weird. All this happening at once. Gotta be UFOs."

"They'll explain it all in time," Gary said. "Get your head back in the car, Liam."

"OK. Yeah. Don't want to get zapped by an alien." Liam shut his window, still peering upward.

"Try to comfort your sister." Nina gave Liam "the look" again. "Make sure she's secure in her seat."

"Anything online?" Gary glanced at the phone Nina had dropped into a cup holder.

She picked it up. "No signal at all."

"Tower probably down. Look, the rain has totally quit. Since I'm a police officer, I should see if I can help." He unbuckled his seat belt and reached for the door handle.

Nina grabbed his arm. "No, Gary! You just admonished Liam for sticking his head out and you want to walk around out there? What if there's an aftershock? It could swallow you."

"It could swallow our car," Liam drawled.

"You're really practicing to be a teenager, aren't you?" Nina glared at him.

A rap on Gary's window halted the argument. He opened it to an older man in a straw hat. "Hello. Everybody okay?" The man tried to stick his head in the window to look around.

"Yes," Gary answered. "Your people?"

"Okay. Some bad wrecks up ahead, though. A lot of injured, I expect. Maybe dead. Your phone working?"

"No. There's no signal," Nina replied. She looked torn, then unbuckled her seat belt. "I'm a nurse. If there are injured I need to help. I'll get the first aid kit." She was out of the car and heading toward the trunk.

Gary looked even more conflicted. "I need to go too. Liam, stay with your sister and take care of her. Be careful of anyone who approaches. I'll shut off the engine and open the windows a bit but I want you to keep the doors locked."

*   *   *

At the high-security government Tech Center deep in the forests of the North Carolina mountains a team sat at computer terminals reviewing and preparing data for transfer. Chris Mills spoke out. "Hey, has anybody seen this story about all the weird weather disasters in the Smokies?"

Jeff Hawke, the team leader, jerked his head toward Chris. "Is Cherokee affected?" As he spoke, he clicked on a news source, scrolling to scan the information.

"Not that I see." Chris looked concerned. Jeff was from Cherokee and still had family there, although he had been away for a number of years, most recently working in cybersecurity at a police headquarters in North Carolina's Research Triangle located in the state's center—the site to which the data they processed was being transferred to restore the network that had been decimated by intruders.

Jeff loudly blew air out his mouth. "That's a relief. But it looks like the Gatlinburg area has been hit hard by fire. Whoa! Reports also of heavy hail, thunderstorms, and an earthquake all at once on 441? What's going on!" In the past months Jeff had experienced fantastic things, yet this rattled him.

Lana Adams sniffed. "Looks like Mother Nature's acting out. Can't blame 'er the way she's being treated."

*   *   *

"Damn! Battery died!" Liam threw his electronic game on the car floor.

"I think that's a bad word," Emma lisped.

"Go back to sleep. Guess that's what I'll do too. Getting boring in here."

It didn't take either child long to fall asleep; then, Emma's eyes shot open abruptly. "Who are you?" Her head swiveled. No one was visible other than the snoring Liam. "Who are you?" She repeated and touched her head. "Are you in there?" A brilliant swath of light beamed around Emma. She turned, her eyes widening. A giggle escaped. "I see you!" she exclaimed. "A fairy! A beautiful fairy."

A soft female voice soothed her. "You like fairies, don't you? Just remember we are good. We will reconnect you. Now sleep peacefully." Emma's eyes closed; she fell into a calm sleep.

As the voice intoned, light pulsed around Emma, colored swirls danced. A phantom emerged, at first with just a gossamer hint of human form, then coalescing into the figure of a young woman sitting on the seat between the two sleeping children. She mused, "Sorry to use you this way, little girl, but you're the strongest link to The Living World around here. Even the natural surroundings are in chaos. I just needed you momentarily to form my Passageway. Now I'll be gone and you might remember a strange dream. I hope a pleasant one. Oops. Gotta do one more trick." She blinked out and then appeared outside the car. "Now, I do hope I can find a more proper Passageway farther into these woods." She marched off into the trees.

■　　■　　■

Nina and Gary helped locate the injured and set up a triage. Unfortunately, several were already dead. Others appeared to be badly hurt. The unhurt were helping in any way they could.

Relief surged through them when two government helicopters set down as close to the wreckage as possible in the Clingman's Dome parking area. All the injured couldn't be evacuated at once; the worse cases went first. They were assured that supplies were en route as well. The earthquake had not affected a large area, so buses could be brought in to eventually evacuate everyone. It would be a long day and night. Wearily, the Goodsen couple trudged back to their car. They found the children in deep sleep and tried to seat themselves without arousing them, but Emma woke up babbling. "Mommy, Daddy, a fairy came to see me!"

"That's wonderful, darling. I'm sure it came to help you," Nina said. "We'll get a snack out of the cooler."

"It was here to help all of us." Emma cooed, "Everything's going to be all right now. They will reconnect us."

Nina and Gary looked sharply at each other. Then Gary laughed. "You've been listening to Liam too much, honey." Both parents chuckled.

"Fairies? Ha! I bet it was aliens! I *would* sleep through that!" Liam was wide awake and ornery.

■　■　■

"Where are you, Mr. MacIntyre?" Annilu was an impatient Synon who didn't much care for visiting Earth, even though Synons were mandated by The Living World with maintaining and nourishing the bond with Earth through Passageways that tethered it to the Synon's Realm. Earth's people were messy, chaotic, illogical. But here she was, having been chosen by TuMa'Aye Gra'Vay, Queen of the Realm herself, for an emergency expedition to investigate what was threatening Earth's link to The Living World. In the formless Realm, Synons existed as connected energy-spirit-mind entities. They had the ability to use their own and ambient energy and matter to form semblances of objects and personas of living creatures. Annilu had used the abundant vegetation surrounding her to reform and enhance her human female body.

Bailey MacIntyre, a Synon who had lived long as a human in the persona of a National Security Agency official, had transmitted that he was near a secret facility in the North Carolina mountains that they would use as their base. It should have been easy to locate him, but Earth had other ideas. The entire globe appeared to be engulfed with earthquakes, tumultuous storms, tornadoes, floods, fires, and other natural disasters. The Passageway Annilu traversed from the Realm had closed abruptly short of her destination on Earth. She had no choice but to create a portal in the first spot where she could find sufficient connection to The Living World to provide the necessary power. Unfortunately, that source had been a five-year-old girl strapped in a car seat in the middle of a massive automotive pile-up caused by natural disasters that had propelled the surrounding natural life into shock so severe that it was unable to provide the necessary power she needed.

Annilu sent soothing thoughts to the child, hoping no harm had come to her, at the same time ensuring that the older brother next to her continued to sleep. Now she hastily scanned her location and found it to be some distance to the west of MacIntyre. As she moved deeper into the forest MacIntyre's signature gradually became clearer. "Got it." she mentally sent. "On my way." Annilu sloughed off the human persona, revealing her own amorphous, slightly glowing self, and moved at near light speed.

*   *   *

The Goodsens were among those whose vehicles were near the earthquake location but not damaged. At the rear terminus of the traffic jam vehicles were being backed out and space created for them to turn around using both lanes of the closed highway. It was a slow, tedious process that sent travelers back where they had come from rather than forward where they wanted to go. Those ahead of the quake were the lucky ones. Eventually they were able to simply drive on toward their destinations. Those like the Goodsens, who were trapped near the dangerous quake fault, were gingerly guided around it to hike to buses parked at Clingman's Dome. They were allowed to only bring a small amount of luggage. Gary had turned over his car keys to the highway patrol, confident that their possessions would be safe. Vehicles that were damaged or destroyed would be towed when the ground was safe, and those like the Goodsens' that could be moved by skilled drivers would be taken somewhere that owners could retrieve them.

The kids were tired and cranky. Gary and Nina's nerves were frayed. They were grateful when the family was comfortably ensconced in a large tour bus commandeered for this mission. They all sank into an exhausted sleep. Night had fallen when they were awoken to learn that they were being deposited at a hotel in Asheville. They hastily settled in and resumed their sleep.

The next morning the room phone woke them with an invitation to complimentary breakfast in the lobby area. "I wonder who's paying for all this," Nina quipped.

"Maybe Homeland or even the Red Cross. They take care of people affected by disasters," Gary suggested.

Many of the people from their bus were at the hotel. Those who lived nearby had found their way home. Since the Goodsens were from Florida, they had to wait for their vehicle.

During breakfast, the refugees were getting acquainted when a commotion in the lobby spilled into the dining room. A television camera crew barged in, past protesting hotel employees. A young Asian woman seemed to be in charge, deploying the crew and carrying a portable microphone. A burly man with a camera on his shoulder followed her.

"Could I have your attention, please?" Her voice rang above the din. "I'm Suki Kurosawa, reporter-producer from the Your Cable News network." A murmur rumbled through the room, then quiet descended. "First, everyone at YCN extends our sorrow for any losses you've suffered. We're happy to see so many of you here, obviously okay. You've been through an ordeal, but sharing might help you to process it. Feel free to speak, and after we finish filming we'll ask you to sign release forms to use your footage. Even though this is a news event, we want to respect your privacy." The group warmed to her, with many nods and some muttered comments of appreciation.

"Who would like to begin? Just tell us what happened to you—when, where you were, and how you felt." Hesitant silence met her invitation.

Greg spoke up. "I'm a police officer on vacation from Florida with my family." He didn't point them out, but Nina looked uncomfortable; Liam preened a bit, and Emma looked perplexed. "We were on U.S. 441 from Gatlinburg late morning. The traffic was heavy with people fleeing the fire behind us. Almost simultaneously, there was a sudden severe storm and an earthquake." The television crew members looked at each other pointedly.

"Are you saying all that happened at the same time?" Kurosawa interjected.

"That's what simultaneous means." Liam cut in.

"I know that. I just need to clarify it. That's a rare occurrence, I believe."

Liam, irritated at the reporter, hijacked the interview, oozing sarcasm. "All at once. I reiterate. Do you know what that means?" He didn't give her a chance to answer. "The fault was just a little way in front of us. Cars, trucks, SUVs, campers were wrecked."

"Was your vehicle damaged?"

"No." Gary took control again, throwing an admonishing look at his son. "Since none of us was hurt, my wife, who's a nurse, and I left the kids in the locked car and went to render aid."

Emma beamed. "Oh! You're telling about our adventure yesterday! I saw a fairy! She visited me in the car!"

Tinkles of laughter rang through the room. Suki at first just smiled at Emma and started to ask Gary another question; then a lightbulb seemed to illuminate above her head. This was a great human-interest twist. People loved cute kids. "What's your name, honey?"

"Emma."

"How old are you?"

Emma held up five fingers.

"Five years old. And a fairy visited you?"

"Oh yes. She talked to me. At first she was just in my head, and then I saw her next to me."

"What did she say?" Suki was grinning as the camera zoomed in on the cute face.

"We're good and we'll reconnect you," Emma stated. That sent a new murmur through the room.

"She said they are good and will reconnect you? With your friends, family? Back home?"

"No. She meant us. All of us. Everybody." More murmurs.

Suki was thrown off but persisted in questioning the child. "What makes you think she meant 'all of us' instead of just you?"

"I just know." Emma fell silent, fidgeting.

"That's enough with my daughter," Nina snapped.

Liam couldn't keep quiet. "She thinks it was fairies, but we all know it was aliens." That brought a round of laughter that elicited a dark scowl from the boy. "You guys know about it, don't you?" He stared at the television crew.

"Liam! Quiet!" Gary's tone was harsher than usual.

After several others had given their interviews they were asked to sign the release forms. Gary agreed to sign, stipulating that under no circumstances were his children to be shown or their names provided.

But Suki Kurosawa had all she needed.

CHAPTER TWO

"Here, kitty, kitty. Cosmos? Come on in; it's getting dark."
Marie LaRue broke into a grin watching the sleek black creature bounding toward her. Her heart seemed to leap as high
as the cat that suddenly was atop the porch railing next to her,
his green eyes narrowing slightly as they gazed up at her in the
feline version of a kiss. "You darling thing," Marie murmured,
snuggling him into her arms and pressing her face against
his silky fur. His purr was louder than the crickets' evening
serenade. How quickly he had acclimated as a mostly indoor
pet, content not to venture beyond the confines of their new
home and its wooded lawn that expanded downward to curve
along the bank of a creek. He had also learned his new name,
Cosmos, rather than the previous "Cat" he had been dubbed by
the Synon queen, TuMa'Aye Gra'Vay, in her human Tami Graves
persona when she first found him surviving in an urban park
at the beginning of the extraordinary events that had brought
them to this point.

Marie and Jeff Hawke had adjusted as well to an abrupt
upheaval involving a quick move from North Carolina's bustling urban Research Triangle to the mountain Tech Center.

Their first sight of what was advertised as a "camp" endeared them to the small log cabin with its wrap-around screened porch. Neither could have given it up, confirming the notion they had been entertaining of cohabitating, after several years of working together as best friends had grown into a stronger bond. The transition from best friends to significant others was almost as smooth as Cat's transition to a pampered house pet. It just seemed natural, with few awkward moments. There was little time to devote to relationship building. Often they were assigned to different time shifts at the facility and found them-selves eager to steal precious time together. The cabin and its setting were an ideal getaway from their intense work.

This was one of those rare times when they would both be at home for an evening. Marie had stopped at the farmers' market for fresh corn on the cob, yellow and zucchini squash, and sweet onions to go with the dried lentils simmering in the crock pot, permeating the house with aromas of herbal seasonings.

She had just fed Cosmos and begun cutting the squash when Jeff called.

"Have you heard what's happening in the Smokies?"

"No. I've been blissfully news free. Is something bad going on?"

He quickly filled her in, then his voice went flat. "And I don't know if this is connected at all but…." His voice trailed off.

"Oh no," she whined, knowing what was coming.

"Yeah. Some bigwigs are arriving for a meeting."

"Tonight?"

"Yeah," he repeated wearily. "Tonight. I'm really sorry. I was looking forward to a nice evening together."

"Me too." She tried to keep the disappointment out of her voice. "I was doing a nice veggie dinner, but it will all keep."

"Go ahead and enjoy it. Just save the leftovers for me. And don't wait up. If it's too late when we wind up I'll just stay in the crash room." The crash room contained bunk beds, recliners, and comfort necessities for personnel use. The nature of the work necessitated unpredictable hours.

* * *

In the North Carolina mountains, as across the country, the interstate highway system brought quicker and safer travel to the nation. It rendered what had been the main, usually two-lane, highways to secondary roads used most often by locals. More obscure roads that were characterized by extreme curves and elevation changes crisscrossed the area, large swaths of which were protected forests, wild and pristine, and the perfect setting to hide a top-secret facility. What was simply called "the Tech Center" was tucked away in such a place. Close enough to the largest mountain city, Asheville, but far enough away that it was nearly impossible for an exploring visitor to stumble upon it.

An old brick building that had once housed a hydroelectric plant perched next to a small lake that had been dammed to power the plant. Water now flowed serenely from a river tributary to the lake by a low waterfall, then continuing on its natural path. At one point the building had been renovated and served as a factory with tall windows on the upper floor while the lower floor retained its unbroken stern brick façade. As the

South's textile industry was flung across the world like a skein of thread with a hollow center, this factory, like so many others, was abandoned through bankruptcy. It had sat unoccupied for several decades until it was quietly scooped up by a clandestine arm of the federal government. Within it now, Jeff Hawke and his team worked with a new kind of thread, skeins of data from the loom of the former Bandela, renegade Synon, now wearing the persona of the young hacker Josh Jackson, imprisoned in his protective Faraday Cage translating code with potential that flabbergasted those who first saw it.

Tami Graves had led her Synons to challenge Bandela inside the municipal cyber system he had hijacked and compromised with indecipherable code. Once he was captured, the most urgent need was to restore that Research Triangle computer network to working order. To accomplish this, the renegade Synon was taken under extreme security to a heavily protected area where high echelon scientists and technicians reviewed and interpreted the data, then securely sent the portions that were relevant to their mission to the Tech Center for final preparation and transmission to its final destination.

■   ■   ■

Three of the five-member tech team were on duty and eating a hastily thrown together dinner in the second-floor break room whose tall windows displayed the western sky in its glorious reds and golds, floating atop a sea of mountains as the sun readied to disappear.

"Does anybody know who's coming to this meeting and why?" Mannie Patel looked at Jeff.

"No," Jeff replied. "We'll find out soon enough. No need to speculate. Enjoy your meal."

"It might be our last for a while," Lana Adams quipped, her dangling earrings chiming accompaniment. "In the immortal words of Han Solo, I've got a bad feeling about this."

"You gonna hit us with some of your low country voodoo predictions now?" One eyebrow arched sardonically as Mannie Patel's sharp New York accent contrasted with Lana's coastal South Carolina drawl. Both broke out into grins. The close-knit team enjoyed mock jabs at each other.

"As I said, no need to ponder. Just eat while you can," Jeff growled, grinning.

Jeff turned out to be the prophetic one at the table. The door burst open and the familiar lined face of Lewis Henderson popped in. Henderson had been friend and mentor to Jeff for years, providing guidance to the young man who had left his Cherokee home for the military and wound up working in IT security for the very Research Triangle police department whose computer network had been Bandela's incursion point. For all those years Jeff had no inkling that the aged Cherokee he called Lew was not a man at all. It had taken time for him to adjust to the revelation of Henderson's true nature—and to that of others he had first known as humans, Tami Graves and Bailey MacIntyre. Lew had joined the Tech Center to continue mentoring Jeff and as a companion to the only other Synon on the team, his pal MacIntyre.

Now Lew was issuing orders. "Cram in what food you can, guys. We got a bevy of Synons straight from the Realm on the way. You got a few minutes. MacIntyre's fetching 'em." Henderson used the term "Synons" in a manner that belied the fact that he was one himself. Jeff was glad the person he still regarded as his old Native American mentor had decided to become a part of their team that would handle whatever their director, MacIntyre, assigned them. With high security clearance, they were among the few humans who were aware of Synons. The door closed. They stared at one another in astonishment for a moment, then followed Henderson's advice and silently shoved food into their mouths. Jeff grabbed his phone to call Chris Mills, the fifth team member, and Marie, to tell her to stow the food and get there. If Synons were coming, everybody needed to be on board for the meeting.

■   ■   ■

The verdant land surrounding the Tech Center nourished The Living World. Bailey MacIntyre had easily found an accessible Passageway through which he ushered the small contingency from The Realm, except for Annilu who had been caught up in Earth's tantrum and separated from the group. They met near a high waterfall gracefully spilling its bounty into a wide pool, skipping over rocks, cascading into a small river. Moss glistened like an emerald carpet laid over gnarled tree roots. From it peeked orange and white mushrooms. Rocks jutted at angles forming shallow caves that echoed the spirits of ancient native dwellers. Majestic trees stood sentinel over shrubs and wildflowers that inexplicably blossomed in vivid colors, despite the lack of direct sunlight within this primeval haven. Annilu felt the presence of innumerable creatures and soaked up the connection with The Living World.

She transformed into her persona, a tall, lithe woman with brown hair pulled back in a ponytail; she wore a dark blue pant suit over a plain white blouse—her idea of a no-nonsense female agent. TuMa'Aye Gra'Vay had shared information on this modern world with the Earthbound Synons, complete with current looks that would never have concerned the focused Annilu but were necessary to succeed in mingling with people. She had also trained them to form lifelike personas that were so fine-tuned they could access sources of phenomena that biological Earth creatures perceived through senses. The other visiting Synons were Tork and Judilay. Tork's esteem and strength would have placed him just below TuMa'Aye Gra'Vay if the concept of rank existed in the Realm. His presence spoke of the importance of this mission. He could be congenial with people but bore a forceful attitude. Tork's persona was a middle-aged man in business attire, fit and distinguished with the aura of someone accustomed to getting his way. Judilay, the third visitor, was in the form of a young man of African descent with hair in elaborate dreadlocks and wearing a vividly colored dashiki over jeans.

Annilu looked at his hairdo and practiced her human derisive snort. "What a lot of precious energy you must waste maintaining that!"

Judilay raised an eyebrow and spoke in his mock sarcastic tone. "Why not add a touch of fun to our mission?" His eyes swept over her. "Your drab look could sure use a makeover."

Tork's expression was not one of amusement.

"Let them get used to it," Bailey MacIntyre drawled with a grin. "Jeff and Marie are the only team members here who have experienced Synons other than me and Henderson. They appreciate originality in persona design. The others will relate to you much easier if you look and act like people they would normally meet. Let's get going. We have a little hike to our vehicle."

The two newbies took in MacIntyre's tall, lean but muscular body, tanned, lined face, and shoulder-length gray hair, which his bushy eyebrows matched.

Tork inhaled deeply. Momentarily dropping his standard formalized manner of speaking. "Great. It's so gratifying to be in this natural wonderland."

They walked to a narrow dirt road on which sat a black SUV.

Judilay's cultivated humor bubbled. "G-man ride! Looks like all those action movies TuMa'Aye funneled into our minds. You're living it to the hilt, aren't you?"

MacIntyre's face slid into a wry grimace. "Gotta live up to the expectations. But it's a fuel-efficient prototype. Get in and enjoy the ride."

Twilight threw shadows as they drove through dense forests along roads that seemed barely there; on one side they teetered on the edge of a steep cliff while the other side was walled-in by the mountain they descended by a narrow, curved road.

As dusk deepened, MacIntyre took the ride as an opportunity to tell his guests about the facility but was interrupted by his phone ringing. He looked at the caller ID and made an exasperated sound as he pressed the green phone icon on his steering wheel. "What'd'ya want, Vera? You know I can't talk to the press." The Synons were politely quiet, looking away, but everyone knew they could sense what the caller said.

Vera ignored him. "What do you know about these catastrophes, Bailey? How should we cover them? We don't want to cause panic, but we have a responsibility to inform the public so they can take the best actions."

MacIntyre answered dryly. "Tell them Mother Nature is having a nervous breakdown."

"I'm serious. What should we suggest that people do?"

"Tell them to monitor their local news and follow instructions from local officials."

"No discussion of the fact that natural disasters are happening everywhere? We just got a report of simultaneous fire, severe storm, and earthquake in the Smoky Mountains. We're trying to get a camera crew there, but it's total chaos and the main highways are affected. We did get someone to Asheville where some survivors were taken."

Annilu nodded her head vigorously in acknowledgment.

Not noticing Annilu, MacIntyre's expression soured. "Don't jump around from place to place showing one disaster after another. That will surely cause panic. Just check with your usual official sources."

"Is there more to this than you're letting on, Bailey? You always know the underside of everything that's going on. Maybe you're just passing the buck to Mother Nature when she's being manipulated somehow."

"Vera, please don't encourage these crazy theories about alien attacks and such. Stick to facts, and when you don't have facts, just be honest. Stress monitoring local news and officials. I know your competitors might run a lot of sensationalized speculation, but your network is trusted for integrity and honesty. Keep it that way. I gotta go now." He disconnected.

His passengers remained politely silent. MacIntyre guffawed. "Okay, guys. Vera Schechner is news director at YCN."

What's that?" Annilu asked.

"Your Cable News, a twenty-four-hour network. I've known her for decades. She's all right. An old-style journalist. She checks in with me when she needs direction to keep people informed without compromising government operations."

"But this is not a government operation," Tork said.

"Why did you tell her that Mother Nature is having a nervous breakdown?" Annilu demanded. "It might seem humorous, but it's too close to the truth to suggest to the media."

"Would they ever believe such a thing?" Judilay retorted. "I recall a human cliché about the truth being stranger than fiction, and I hope they don't figure this one out."

"A few of them will," Tork said. "But they'll be ignored as crazies."

■　■　■

When Jeff learned that their guests were Synons he had the team prepare the conference room by powering up the tech equipment and making coffee for themselves. The team was anxious about meeting new Synons. They were used to Bailey MacIntyre and Lewis Henderson but found the notion of newly arrived Synons exciting. They even discussed if they'd be able to discern any kinks in their human personas and behavior, as if it would be a game.

"We need to make them feel comfortable and welcome," Jeff reminded them.

At that moment Lewis Henderson strolled in, grinning slightly. "Hyped about meeting some newbies?"

The group fidgeted and looked guilty. Henderson laughed. "If they could be nervous, they would be. Just treat them the way you do Mac and me."

"Like Vulcans?" Chris piped up. He was a sci-fi geek and loved having supernatural beings around who were human enough that he could tease them.

Henderson draped his lanky body into a chair. "They wouldn't be here if we weren't facing a crisis," he said soberly, changing the mood. "You should feel honored that they selected this site for the meeting, and have included you. They could have just used the facility and told you to go home."

The door opened and MacIntyre escorted the three new "people" in. He introduced everyone to each other and the newcomers were seated. The tech team had automatically sat at one end of the table facing each other, leaving the end chair free. Henderson sank into it. MacIntyre sat in the middle of the table next to Jeff with Tork on one side of him and Judilay and Annilu across from them next to Marie. After introductions, the room fell into silence. Jeff was just as amazed at the individual details of these three personas as he was with all those he had previously met, especially Tami Graves, whom he still had trouble accepting as a Synon. It had taken some theatrics and a crisis for Tami, MacIntyre, and Henderson to convince him that they weren't human. Now he was looking at three strangers, all of whom looked and behaved like people. The thought about Tami Graves evoked conflicting emotions that Jeff would have preferred stay buried.

MacIntyre, ever the showman, soaked it up a moment, then spoke. "We are honored to have these three esteemed guests, and I wish it were merely for a pleasure trip. But we all know it's not.

We're especially honored to have Tork with us, whom we should call TuMa'Aye Gra'Vay's right hand. I'd like to turn the floor over to him."

Tork rose and smiled. "First, the queen sends her warmest regards to you. She said she would enjoy visiting with you but felt she should remain in the Realm to oversee the unfolding events on Earth and coordinate Synon responses." He sat down, placed his elbows on the table, and leaned forward in a less formal posture.

Jeff again felt the rush of old feelings, now overlaid with bitterness. Tami Graves had stalked him, plundered information from his mind, and fashioned herself as "the woman of his dreams." The renegade Synon incursion into his city's cyber network had forced him to work with her after Tami's startling revelation about her true nature. He developed a healthy awareness that for Synons their purpose was paramount and their human impersonations were designed to that end. Jeff appreciated the opportunities his association with these creatures had provided him, and he fully understood why their purpose always took precedence; its importance could not be understated. Yet his emotional side still felt ill used.

Tork continued, more relaxed. "MacIntyre says you've been sequestered here focusing on your mission and that no unusual natural events have taken place in the nearby area. Your knowledge of what is happening has probably been from fleeting reports so that you likely do not have a full grasp of its scope."

The team looked at one another. Jeff spoke for them. "Until today when it hit so near, we'd snatched some news snippets about natural disasters all over the world, much more prevalent than normal. We know global warming and climate change are playing havoc with the weather and have just sort of attributed it to that. We *are* pretty absorbed in our work."

Tork nodded. He looked at each team member in turn, then spoke gravely. "Global warming does have a detrimental effect. It will worsen if people continue to do so little. I sense a bit of despair in all of you, as if you feel we are in a downward spiral that can't be curbed. Unfortunately, that sentiment is in the minority. Many people find ways to rationalize their attitudes and behavior by saying that what happens to the earth is natural. They don't want to face the necessary changes in their lives to mitigate it."

The group looked at each other again, wondering where Tork was going.

"You are among the very, very few humans who will hear this information. We know you can be trusted to keep it in the strictest confidence, as confidential as the work you do here."

They squirmed a bit. Someone cleared their throat. All nodded emphatically and murmured affirmation. Jeff felt a weight bearing down on him. They were still overwhelmed with the "Bandela" project and now were to be, at the least, the recipients of secret and dire information.

Tork turned pedantic. "People metaphorically use the terms Mother Earth and Mother Nature. We of the Realm know that the Earth is a living being, part of The Living World. This is an ancient concept among people, of course, and some today do believe it. But most scoff at the notion. I assure you that it is true."

The team exchanged glances again. Chris couldn't contain his glee. "I knew it!" He grinned.

Tork smiled at him. "You certainly belong here," he said. "Now I'll explain more. We call Earth 'her' to follow the metaphor. You could say she's an organism intrinsically linked with the biology, ecosystems, and natural rhythms that comprise what we know as life here. Like you, she has an immune system that protects her from invading enemies. For you, it's viruses, bacteria, etcetera. For her the invader is the human species, which is beginning to threaten her future by disrupting the balance of vital components that support life. To put it simply, she is fighting back. This notion is not alien to human discourse. It has been considered recently and has appeared in literature and even some scientific theories. But we Synons can faithfully say that just like your immune system fights off a cold with a runny nose and coughing, or a stomach virus elicits violent bodily reactions, Earth is fighting back with her own symptoms: disruptions in weather, tectonic plate activity, and so forth, going beyond the damage caused by humans. She is so preoccupied that she's totally withdrawn. We can't communicate with her."

"Can you normally?" Jeff asked, feeling the hairs on his neck rising.

"Yes. That's what has us so concerned."

Marie blurted, "What about The Living World? I'm a bit confused about the lines of…kinship, but isn't The Living World the over-powering force? Can't it communicate with everything?" She shrugged. "I apologize if I'm offensive in any way."

Mannie Patel stood up, glaring at Tork. He spoke quietly and evenly. "Isn't The Living World in charge?"

"We are all interdependent. The links aren't direct and linear but radiating and inclusive. If one element of the link weakens it affects the entirety. Like individual entities, planets, galaxies, the components of this universe are born and die naturally."

Mannie had taken his seat, his demeanor changed. "They don't commit suicide." Mannie said quietly. "Not until now."

Tork nodded gravely at Mannie. "You are perceptive. This situation is much more dire than any person on Earth realizes. And we are the ones who have to fix it."

CHAPTER THREE

Not long after breakfast the Goodsens got word that their vehicle wouldn't be delivered until the following day. They decided to sightsee, but it was difficult to settle on something a preschooler and a twelve-year-old would both like. Liam was disappointed at having missed Cherokee; an exhibit of Native American items was on display at the Asheville Art Museum, within walking distance of their hotel. A children's area was available, so Nina and Emma checked that out while Liam and Gary went to the Cherokee exhibit. Afterwards, they had lunch nearby and returned to the hotel for a rest. As soon as they entered their room, Liam turned on the television to YCN.

"Liam, we need some quiet so that Emma can nap." Nina was about to switch the set off when the face of the YCN reporter who had interviewed them flashed on, followed by a shot of their hotel dining room. "Lookee! It's us!" Emma ran and touched the screen.

Gary's face tightened. "They had better not show—"

"Shhh!" She's talking about us!" Liam sat on the floor in front of the set.

The Asian reporter's face again filled the screen as she spoke directly into the camera. "The harrowing tales of fear and struggle were punctuated by a reminder of the resilience of children." Gary sucked in his breath, reaching for the remote.

"Wait, Dad!" Liam held up his hand. Gary exhaled in a loud sigh and sat on the foot of a bed, glaring at the screen.

The reporter was speaking excitedly. "…power of children's imagination to transport them from a potentially terrifying experience to a fanciful adventure. Here's an example. An adorable child insisted that a fairy had visited and talked with her, while her older brother was equally adamant that it had been an alien." She smiled. "The world of play is never too far from the world of the everyday." Her face took on a sober, contemplative look. "But. Something that child said stuck with me because it sounded so adult, so unlike her normal speech. She said…." A dramatic pause as she peered into the camera. "She said they'd *reconnect us*. That's the words she used. Reconnect us. She went on to say that *us* meant everyone. All of us." Another pause for emphasis. "I have to admit, that chilled me. Out of the mouths of babes. Food for thought? Suki Kurosawa for YCN." Loud music blared from the speakers as a commercial began.

Gary grabbed the remote and turned off the set, throwing Nina a troubled look. "Well, she kept her word not to use the kids' names or faces."

Liam was already scrolling his tablet like a madman. "Whoa! We're famous. With no one even knowing who we are! Everybody's tweetin' that we saw aliens! Gonna check the other sites."

Gary snatched the tablet. "Fair warning, Liam. This is serious. Do not post anything. And I mean *anything* that could link our family to these reports. You have no idea what a mess it could create for us."

"Yeah, I do. We'd be famous. Us." Liam laughed. "And I didn't even see the alien. It was the little squirt. Who'd believe a little kid like her anyway?"

Gary had shut off the tablet and put it in his own backpack. "You're cut off. Just chill. Let's all take a short nap, then we'll go someplace nice for dinner."

Sulking, Liam lay on the bed and turned his back on the room.

Their naps were interrupted by a call that their vehicle was ready. They opted to get on the road. It would be good to get home.

■   ■   ■

Bailey MacIntyre paced around the small room, shouting at the phone sitting on a corner table in speaker mode. "Well, the buck does stop with you, Vera! How the hell did you let her insinuate like that! Everybody's picked it up now, and the whole world is swirling with crazy rumors that we're under alien attack!"

"She was live and went off script. I fired her. Of course, she's already fielding lucrative offers. For what it's worth I'm running an onscreen and online editorial repudiating the implications. But nobody will pay a whit of attention to it." There was a long silence. Bailey continued to pace, deep in thought. "Bailey? I'm just thinking. Maybe this can work to your advantage. Keep the media stirred up chasing aliens and they'll stay away from the obvious—that the earth is having a nervous breakdown."

"That's just a joke that's caught on," Bailey snapped. "Scientists are coming together from all different fields and around the world to share ideas in search of concrete evidence to explain their theories. They'll chase their tails a long time. Time is what we need."

"I'll try to cover that angle. It will ease some people a bit to know the best minds on the planet are looking for answers. But the hordes of science-deniers will still turn to alternate rumors. They'd rather believe outlandish claims of alien invasions than any mention of human activity affecting the climate."

■　■　■

"Our quiet, secluded life here didn't last long, huh?" Marie poured coffee into the large pottery mug sitting on the rough-hewn wooden table in front of Jeff. Early daylight filtered through the trees. A brisk breeze wafted across the porch. Both wore thick bathrobes as they sat savoring the moment.

"I can't believe that I've been drafted to babysit fledgling Synons," he growled.

Marie chuckled. "Annilu and Judilay are hardly fledglings. They've probably been around for eons."

"Fledgling humans, then." He took a large gulp of coffee. "Seems like they'd be better off herded by one of the experienced Synons. I mean, Lew and Mac are human to me and everyone else, but they're still Synons." Jeff and the team had given Bailey MacIntyre the nickname "Mac."

"Well, we have to give them credit for accrued wisdom, Jeff. I think they feel like these two who are a bit inexperienced at playing human need a real human guide. It shows how much trust and confidence they have in you."

He grimaced and took another gulp.

Marie tried to reassure him. "The team can easily handle the work here. It's really become routine. We can set aside anything that needs more attention, and that would probably be for Mac or someone else from NSA anyway. I'm actually kind of jealous that you get to go gallivanting all over the world while I'm stuck here. Albeit in paradise." She smiled wistfully as Cosmos jumped into her lap and nestled. "Sweetie, don't get comfy. We have to go to work." She stroked the silky fur and gently dislodged him as she stood.

Jeff remained seated, still sipping coffee. "I wonder why they didn't send one of the younglings with Tork," he groused. "Then I'd only have one to deal with."

"Tork is as strong as the two of them combined, I think. He can communicate with Earth alone while the other two probably need each other to garner enough power. I'm just surmising, of course. I'm still trying to get my head around the Earth being an entity to talk to."

"People have been doing it forever, in metaphorical or spiritual terms," Jeff replied. "I guess the name The Living World means just that. Everything is alive. So I guess we've been rubbing Earth the wrong way these last couple of centuries with whatever we've been saying. Certainly what we've been doing."

"You'll have the adventure of a lifetime, Jeff!" Marie hugged his seated figure from behind the chair. "We better get dressed and over there."

He reluctantly put his mug down and rose, standing a moment to soak up the ambience of his home. "I'll have to pack some stuff when I find out where we're going. Of course, we could be sent from the Arctic to the Amazon. Might be asking you to overnight me clothes. Or maybe I can get my companions to just reassemble the ones I have to fit the climate." He turned and started inside, with one more look back over his shoulder, as a shaft of sunlight burned brightly onto the creek, wrapping it in a golden glow.

■　■　■

Annilu and Judilay were as apprehensive as Jeff, in as far as they experienced emotion. Both had been to Earth previously, but their human personas had primarily taken on an observational role, with little to no human interaction. Judilay was more eager to mingle with people. He found their contradictions fascinating and wanted to learn more about how they ticked.

Now they again sat in the conference room with a much smaller group than before: the two of them, Tork, Jeff with his ubiquitous coffee, Lewis Henderson, and Bailey MacIntyre. Even as inexperienced as they were, they could see that Jeff Hawke was not happy. He sat staring down at his coffee mug and barely muttered a morning greeting.

Judilay felt a sense of something he identified as akin to guilt. They were wrenching Jeff away from his life to guide a couple of other-worldly beings. Annilu sat impassively. She needed to practice facial expressions and body language, Judilay thought. Maybe he could give her some tips—if she didn't find it insulting.

MacIntyre was speaking, "Tork has suggested that Earth might be more receptive if the attempts to communicate were made at tranquil, unspoiled spots rather than the epicenter of natural disasters."

"That makes sense," Jeff said flatly. He looked a bit relieved.

"I agree," Annilu stated.

Judilay grinned. "Tork knows best."

Tork spoke briskly, ignoring their comments. "In the interest of time and resources, we will try not to travel so far for our initial attempts. I can move very simply, drawing no attention. I'll take the longer trip, as I know how to find and use Passageways to shorten the journey, even though they could be difficult to locate. We all know that an added dimension to this crisis is the deliberate closing of Passageways by Earthdwelling Synons who want to remain hidden here with no interference from the Realm, an issue that the queen continues to address. I'll go to the Everglades in Florida. People don't venture deep into its center, and it's still in a relatively primeval state. Jeff can lead Annilu and Judilay deeper into the mountains. He is familiar with the region. Even though disasters have recently hit nearby, they seem to have been limited to the heavily developed tourist corridor."

Judilay noticed an immediate uplift in Jeff's demeanor and mood. Jeff displayed a slight smile as he spoke. "There are protected forests all around us. People seldom venture off the well-trod trails. In the guise of primitive campers, we can work with rangers to find the best entry points, then move off the trails as much as we need to. I'll get the latest maps. Being human, I'll need to take some supplies and survival gear." He grinned. "I might have to load you two up with my stuff, and you'll need to take enough for yourselves to make you look like real campers. When we get deep in, if you want to go *au natural* at any time,

I'm good with that. I've seen it. Just dump my stuff with me and go to it."

Judilay was disappointed. He had hoped to visit some exotic locale among people and have what the humans called an adventure. Annilu simply nodded. He knew she just wanted to get it over with and preferred less human interaction.

Tork gazed at his two companion Synons. "I suggest that both of you alter your personas to better suit the location for your mission. You will be no-nonsense nature lovers. Athletes who can hike, survivalists in the wild."

Judilay was jubilant. "Oh! I saw this guy on TV last night who was a survival expert. He was demonstrating how to survive in the wilderness. I'll be like him! He had long blond hair and wore some kind of cool vest and lots of leather." He began to shimmer as if about to transition.

"Not now!" Tork barked.

Jeff was laughing. "I think I know who you mean. The ladies find him irresistible, I understand. I can help both of you with research on attire and gear."

Judilay swung his locks. "I'll save this persona for another time. Hate to give it up, but duty calls."

"You'll continue to find ways to be what humans call a peacock," Annilu remarked without humor.

Everyone else laughed.

▪   ▪   ▪

Jeff left the meeting with his spirits considerably higher. He didn't relish the notion of taking these two Synons deep into the forest, but at least their contact with other people would be minimal. He immediately began researching catalogs, photos, and videos of wilderness backpackers and gear. Annilu and Judilay had assured Jeff that they could fabricate proper appearing equipment, which they could make much lighter than the actual thing. They didn't like the idea of having to extend their power to carrying his stuff. That meant he had to haul everything for himself. The personal equipment he owned was probably sufficient, so his main task was making sure his charges were able to make their assertions reality. His supplies were a paramount issue. He planned to gather them while the "kids," as he wanted to call them, studied the research material and prepared themselves. They would set out the following morning. He tried to put himself in the mindset of a Boy Scout troop leader. Leading supernatural creatures posing as humans. To have a heart-to-heart chat with Earth herself. It was serious, but at the same time seemed ridiculous.

■   ■   ■

Tork had been to Earth many times, witnessing humanity progress to its present state. He had interacted with many people across the globe. He felt comfortable and confident in his abilities. But this trip was different than any prior one. Earth had always been the Realm's ally in its quest to help humans develop and maintain strong connections with The Living World. Now Earth had withdrawn from the web of awareness within which Synons functioned. She was acting in an isolated, self-protective mode that Tork must reverse.

Tork set out at dusk for the Florida Everglades. Traveling at night down the Appalachians and then into the backlands of lower Georgia to central Florida he was able to jump along an encouraging number of Passageways. It was beautiful country populated by myriad plants and animals forming unique eco-systems. Undeveloped areas were crisscrossed with roads and punctuated by towns.

It was still dark when he reached the northern terminal of the turnpike that cut a strip through the peninsula from north-central Florida to the door of the Everglades. Hidden in the darkness behind a rest area, Tork formed a new persona, a young, casually dressed man with a ball cap and backpack. He blended in with the people in the snack bar, crowded despite the pre-dawn hour. Weary travelers lining up for coffee included seasoned truckers and bedraggled tourists, including a few whining children. He didn't need physical sustenance, of course, so he hung back soaking up the atmosphere to enhance his persona.

Above the counter a television showed a map of the western Atlantic Ocean featuring a swirling graphic. The narrator spoke of hurricane hunter planes flying into a storm to gather data on its potential strength and direction. It appeared to be heading toward Central America. No one seemed to take notice of the report, but Tork did. Another one of Mother Nature's tantrums? Of course, it was hurricane season. While this storm would prob-ably go elsewhere, he'd need to follow weather reports closely.

Tork felt something tugging at his "jeans." He didn't need to actually look down, but his well-honed persona instincts did. A small girl clung to him, her upturned face wearing a bright smile. "Hello, Mr. Fairy!" she chimed. Tork froze. He knew the child hadn't mistaken him for an acquaintance with the sur-name of "Fairy." His mind had touched hers instantaneously.

He smiled, sending reassurance to her. "Hello there. I think you've mistaken me for someone else," he said softly.

"No! I know you're a fairy. Just like the lady who visited me in the mountains."

Light speed connections reminded him of Annilu's tale of having to use the power of a little girl to form a Passageway. He was certain that this was the same child.

She was babbling at her father, who had grabbed her, lifting her protectively into his burly arms. "Sorry, mister. She can't sleep and is keyed up." His trained police gaze swept appraisingly over Tork. "Emma, leave the man alone."

"No, Daddy. He's a fairy like the lady in the car. I told you. I told the TV lady."

Her father shrugged. "She's in that fairy tale phase. Everybody is some kind of magical being to her."

Tork laughed with him, all the while gently probing the girl's mind. He found her encounters with Annilu and the television reporter. But he also found much more. As her father whisked her away, Tork noticed an adolescent boy glaring at him. Her brother, who turned and stalked off before Tork could attempt to see inside his mind. Tork strolled outside to take note of the license tag on their vehicle as they drove away. This was no ordinary family.

■　■　■

The highway whined with the high-pitched noise of constant traffic. It was easy for Tork to camouflage himself and clandestinely hitch rides in the beds of trucks. As his unwitting drivers sped him toward his destination, the experience prompted him to ponder human transportation. Admittedly, they had invented effective ways to travel, although the trains he'd seen in other locales seemed much more efficient than cars. Most dismaying was the sight of the victims left in the wake of speeding vehicles, animals who had innocently wandered into the path of these killing machines that had invaded their homes. The internal combustion engine still reigned, despite more than a century passing in which it could have been replaced. Its fossil fuel consumption was contributing to pollution and dangerous climate change. Tork wondered if humans could reverse this course in time.

By dawn Tork was close to Lake Okeechobee, so large it was often referred to as an inland sea, even though it was freshwater. Historically, it had been the source of freshwater replenishment, from waterways flowing southward from central Florida to the Everglades at its southern drainage. Human tinkering had changed the dynamics of the natural flows. Over half of the original Everglades had been devoured by drainage, farms, and urban incursion. People had shown enough sense to declare what remained of the Everglades a protected national park, and many dedicated themselves to its sensitive and unique ecosystems. Now the Everglades was seen by most as a vast swamp, populated by alligators, snakes, and other exotic animals, and low grasses. Actually, as the only authentic tropical forest in the northern hemisphere, the area was rich in a variety of life, including over one thousand plant species and hundreds of different birds, reptiles, mammals, and fish.

When the truck whose bed he'd been traveling in stopped for a break, Tork managed to slip out and into dense vegetation. He still had quite a journey to reach his desired position, but it was time to leave highways and human personas behind and move within nature. A bird would be the most efficient creature to emulate, but flight was a complicated process and difficult to maintain. During that day he took many different forms, basking in total immersion with animal and plant energy. It invigorated and elated him.

CHAPTER FOUR

Dawn came much too soon for Jeff. Trying not to waken Marie, he quietly readied himself for the day. Even though no forest fires were close enough to endanger his mission, the acrid taste and stench of smoke hung in the air. He wondered if "the kids" would be aware of it. Could they perceive the way human senses did?

When he reached the facility parking area he saw them patiently waiting for him. Eager beavers. They had changed their appearance. Annilu appeared as a stocky, muscular female wearing an unattractive face and clothing right out of the research material he's supplied. Judilay was almost the spitting image of the blond TV wilderness guide he had gushed about at the meeting. Both carried appropriate looking gear. Both cheerfully greeted him.

"We're going into a national forest, so we'll check in at a ranger station first. It's always best to let them know when you're going in, especially for overnight, and give them a good idea of your planned itinerary."

Annilu piped up. "What if they decide to check on us right when we're trying to commun—"

Judilay cut her off. "What are the odds of that? We can do it in the middle of the night."

Great. Bickering kids. This was going to be a real fun trip. "Let's get going." Jeff tried not to sound as grumpy as he felt.

The ranger station was an information center with a picnic area and trail heads.

Annilu surveyed the array of tourist items for sale as well as the small exhibit of local wildlife and plants. "Isn't this too open and busy? I thought we were going way off the beaten track."

"We will. This is a good place to look at a big exhibit map and get some trail maps to take with us. It's probably best if you just let me do the talking," Jeff replied.

They examined a large three-dimensional topographical map of the western North Carolina mountains. Jeff pointed out Mount Mitchell, the highest point east of the Mississippi River at 6,684 feet above sea level, and showed them Mount Pisgah, 5,721 feet, closer to where they were and where the Tech Center was in relation to his destination.

"I'm in such awe," Judilay murmured. "These are among the oldest mountains on Earth. I love the graceful sweep of ridges contrasted with the valleys. How magnificent."

Jeff was touched by the demeanor of this ancient supernatural creature who had such a unique connection with the Earth. He could think of no appropriate words for a reply. His opinion of Judilay was growing more positive.

"Need some help?" a young female ranger was gazing up at Judilay as if he were Adonis himself.

"Oh, hi." Jeff quickly tried to take control. "Yes. We're going on an overnight hike up into waterfall country. I've been there before but need the latest maps and any pertinent information on current conditions."

She didn't take her eyes off Judilay. "Uh, yes. I can help with that." She blushed. "I just have to ask, are you that TV wilderness guide?"

Judilay basked in her attention. He grinned broadly and answered before Jeff could butt in. "So many people ask me that. I'm flattered, but I'm not even sure who it is you refer to."

Jeff addressed the ranger. "If you or another ranger has time, I'd like to go over some possible routes with you and get maps. We plan to be gone overnight, hopefully back before nightfall tomorrow."

"But what if we can't—" Annilu began.

Jeff cut her off. What was she about to say? How much self-control did these two really have?

"We can move to another location later this week if we want to. For now, let's plan this trek."

"Are you experienced wilderness backpackers?" The ranger looked them over.

"Oh sure! Jeff's Cherokee!" Judilay exclaimed proudly.

The ranger turned fresh eyes on Jeff and liked what she saw, forgetting Judilay. "Oh. That's good to know."

They reviewed all the trails that might work and located the nearest parking area to their trail head. Jeff needed to focus. His life depended on preparations. But his awareness was divided. These rookie Synons could blurt out anything.

Settled on a route, Jeff asked about any specific directives.

"Bears," the ranger said flatly. "Always a possibility, but there have been several sightings recently. Be sure you know exactly what to do."

The two Synons looked at each other and smiled slyly. "Bears will not be a problem for us," Judilay boasted.

Jeff just glared at him. "Healthy respect for Mother Nature's creatures keeps people alive." He arched an eyebrow at Judilay. "I'll coach you on the way to the trail head."

The ranger was disappointed that Judilay's behavior was so different from the television survival guide he so resembled. He and the female seemed like amateurs. She didn't envy the Cherokee herding them into the forest. She found herself wondering why they were going and what the relationships among them were. They seemed ill-matched. She gave them a stern look. "Another warning. Don't take chances on or around waterfalls. Every year there are fatalities when people venture too close to the edge or fall on slippery rocks. Take every step with extreme caution."

Jeff gave her a grateful smile. "Thank you."

A sigh of relief escaped Jeff as he led the "kids" to the vehicle. "I told you to keep your mouths shut," he growled. "Once we get on the trail, keep it totally zipped unless I ask you a direct question. You might be supernatural, but I'm human and all kinds of things can happen to me out there."

"We'll protect you." Annilu said confidently.

■　■　■

After experiencing the glory of numerous varied and majestic falls, including one which cascaded three levels, they trudged along quietly in single file, each seemingly lost in thought. The two Synons were clearly in close communication with the surrounding wildlife. Even though they had mentioned at the falls that it was almost like mental overload at times, they found it exhilarating and encouraging.

The first night the two Synons eagerly offered to help Jeff with his food, clean up, and bedding down, almost as if they were anxious for him to go to sleep. As he snuggled into his bedroll, it dawned on him that they were anxious for good reason. They needed relief from the twin burdens of maintaining their personas and at the same time brushing minds with countless animals and plants during a long day. Then it hit him: of course! They wanted to fulfill their mission in the depths of night, while he slept. That brought an unexpected sense of disappointment; he wanted to witness it. Well, he thought, maybe it won't work if a human is there. I'll ask them in the morning, if they don't say we can just go home because it's all taken care of. Sleep overtook him.

Jeff slept fitfully and awoke to a shaft of bright sunlight boring through the trees right into his eyes. Still half in a vivid dream, he at first was disoriented, and it took a few seconds to recall where he was. The music of birds and the rush of a distant waterfall mixed with pungent forest scents delightfully reminded him of his location. His nose discovered another aroma, bacon, and Indian fry bread. He sat up and looked around. The two Synons sat on rocks next to the fire pit, talking and laughing and tending his breakfast.

"Good morning!" Judilay grinned brightly.

"Good morning," Jeff replied, approaching them, wearing a confused expression. "I didn't bring that food with me."

"You like this, don't you?" Annilu cocked an eyebrow.

"Yes, but…where did it come from?"

"Note that vegetarian bacon smells just like that from a sacrificed porcine." Annilu pointed at what looked and smelled like pork bacon.

"Yeah, Marie introduced me to it. Not bad."

"Lovely lady." Judilay noted. "We found it creative to take nature's residue from around the forest and fashion it into food you would enjoy. Try it." He used a fork made from a twig and placed the food onto a plate that looked suspiciously like a thick leaf.

Jeff was dumbfounded. "You went to all this trouble just for me?"

"It's not trouble. You're our friend and guide. This is a gift." Judilay smiled, holding out the plate.

"Well, I really appreciate it." Jeff took the plate, sat on a rock, and took a taste. He was genuinely touched at this remarkable gesture. "Amazing!" he exclaimed. "It's delicious." He crammed more into his mouth. Once he could speak again he drawled with a grin, "Where's the coffee?"

The two Synons looked at each other. "Oh. We totally forgot that." Annilu looked pained. "We'll get it from your backpack."

She moved toward Jeff's gear but stopped abruptly just as Judilay jumped up, turning toward the densest part of the forest around the small primitive campsite.

"Bear?" Judilay whispered. Just beyond the trees a large, barely visible black figure lumbered toward them.

Jeff's eyes followed as he absently recalled why he had been about to lecture his charges on the reason not to cook food there. The aroma attracted local attention. "Quietly get the pot and my metal cup and bang them together loudly," he said in a low voice.

Ignoring him, both Synons glided toward the animal, locking gaze with the creature as it neared the clearing. Oh no, Jeff thought. They're trying their Synon mind meld. He crouched and crawled to the backpack, rummaging as quietly as he could until he found the metal objects and withdrew them. The bear was curious. It approached the Synons, sniffing loudly. Suddenly, it reared onto its hind legs. Jeff clanged the cup against the pot and yelled. "Make a lot of noise but don't run!"

The bear advanced toward the two figures that now shimmered and glowed as they transformed. Sparks flew toward the confused animal. It turned and fled.

"Are you all right?" Jeff managed. His heart was still pounding.

The Synons had regained their personas but not their composure. They looked forlornly at each other and turned to face Jeff. "We're intact," Annilu said flatly.

Judilay was distraught. He paced and began to rant. "How do we expect to communicate with Earth herself if we can't even get through to a bear?"

Jeff felt a pang of compassion for them. "Not my business, but how did you try to talk to the bear?"

Annilu straightened. "We tried to soothe it with the love of The Living World. To ask it to please move on and not harm this human who was a friend to it and all creatures, just as we are."

"Maybe that was a mistake," Jeff mused. "Wild animals don't always respond to the soft touch. They respond to power. You have to scare bears, like you finally did with the sparks."

But Judilay was right. How could they influence Earth if they couldn't persuade a bear to leave them alone? What if Earth was more like a wild animal than a human or Synon? This mission could be doomed.

■　■　■

As Tork moved farther into the Everglades, he left behind the shrieking air boats that skimmed over swamp water carrying loads of howling humans. His connection to the natural world grew so strong that he could barely contain his fervent desire to shrug off his human persona and merge with this vibrant life in his own natural form. He had not seen or heard any signs of people in hours. He forced himself to wait patiently until dark. People sometimes fished along the edges of the wetlands after dark, but no one would be foolish enough to venture this far into the Everglades at night. Tork was ancient and wise, but as dusk approached he finally ignored the last vestiges of caution and let his true self emerge. His aura flashed like the Aurora Borealis as he transformed. It was as glorious as any experience he had ever had. A moment to savor forever. He felt like a frolicking young animal. He was one with countless creatures of the land, air, and water. They sang with him: the croaks of frogs, foghorn roars of alligators, chirps of birds, but no growl of a panther, driven to near-extinction by humans.

This had to be the time. Tork thrust his mentality deep into the water, communing with myriad life forms, reaching deeper, deeper. He visualized the molten center of the earth and marveled at this living planetary organism.

Tork suddenly brushed sentience, vast but faint. He was drenched in pain. Impressions flitted through his consciousness: torment, illness, despair, helplessness. Earth helpless!

He sent a fervent plea. "How can the Realm aid you?"

No words answered him; only continued impressions surfaced through the misery: Invasive species. Destruction.

"Humans? Destroying you?"

A sense of affirmation.

"Can you control your defensive actions at all?"

Barely.

"The combination of human destruction and your uncontrollable responses are hastening catastrophe."

Sorrowful acknowledgment.

He repeated his question. "How can we help?"

Only they can help.

"Synons?"

No response.

"The Renegade Synons who are abandoning the Realm and closing Passageways?"

No response.

"Humans?"

Abruptly he was alone. All sense of Earth's presence had vanished.

Tork lingered a long time in the same spot, surrounded by nocturnal life. He touched many beings, but the link with Earth herself had severed.

The wind began to whip through the grasses and trees in gales that sprang to sudden life only to abruptly subside. Downpours followed in concert like a symphony. The dormant waters rose in waves like jutting mountain peaks.

There was no shelter for Tork. He gathered his being tightly together, then wound it around the trunk of a huge bald cypress tree whose knotty roots scrambled in all directions like lines on a map, driving deep into the water on whose edge it lived. Large protruding hunks of root looked like sculptures strung along the tree's base. They provided a secure place for Tork's energy-mind-spirit to cling to this ancient entity, asking for its protection and feeling its assurance grasping him. Hours passed as the hurricane raged.

*   *   *

Everyone, including the meteorological community, was caught off guard by the quick turn and strengthening of an obscure storm in the Atlantic that no computer models had shown posing any threat to the U.S. mainland. Now it raged onshore in south Florida with a direct hit on the Everglades so quickly that the scattered residents and visitors in the area scrambled to evacuate. Some had been outside looking for the flashes of swirling, colored lights that had reportedly been seen. They reached shelters wild-eyed, exchanging tales and ratcheting up the rumor toll. The lights and the sudden storm had to be connected. It might well be aliens. In all the movies their arrival disrupted natural forces.

*   *   *

Once the storm passed Tork was shaken. Wary that people searching for survivors or surveying damage might encounter him, he returned to his human persona and began making his way through the debris left in the hurricane's wake. What he saw flabbergasted him. It looked as if a furious giant had rampaged pulling up huge trees and flinging them. He sensed frightened animals hiding. Small fish camps and cabins were smashed. He did see a few people so stunned that they merely nodded at him with blank stares as they stumbled amid the debris.

Tork trudged as a man would, watching his step as he sought out the driest ground, littered with huge clumps of soil, uprooted grass, and other vegetation. A human would have to be careful, indeed, in this environment in which deadly residents certainly lurked. He thought mostly of alligators but was surprised to almost step on a huge boa constrictor. Boa constrictors had become an invasive species in the Everglades. They were not native, but their population had increased from "pet" snakes set loose in the swamp by owners no longer able or willing to care for them. It proved a lucrative environment for the reptiles. Tork had never encountered one of these creatures, but this one was suddenly aware of and staring right at him, obviously contemplating how to strike. It fascinated Tork, and he worked to touch its mind. The sharp predatory focus was a formidable barrier. Tork realized the snake was confused by his lack of human scent. He decided to remove the visual prey he represented by transforming into his natural state. That process, in turn, fascinated the snake, who attacked the shimmering specter before it. Momentarily, Tork feared that his ancient existence was about to be ended by being compressed and digested by one of earth's most primal beings. As his persona's matter transformed into energy it took all his skill to funnel it out of reach of the grasping reptile. Its very presence in this unlikely place spoke of humanity's cavalier attitude toward living things. Baby animals of all sorts were cute and attractive to them, but as they grew and required more attention and resources people discarded their pets just like they did inanimate objects they had grown tired of. At least those who had thrown their pet boas into the Everglades had attempted to give them a chance to continue living, but it illustrated the shortsighted and shallow thinking that seemed to characterize the current state of humanity.

Tork remained in his natural form, soaring over the wreckage that spread outward to towns and cities. Had the Earth sent that hurricane as a direct message to him? If so, he truly hoped that no life had been lost. That would be a burden that would forever bear down on him. The human term "despair" was palpably clear to him now. It certainly described the Earth as well as his own state after her rebuke of his attempt at communication. Mother Earth had spewed her own venom across the landscape. He despaired that it might be too late to reach her. Reluctantly, he reached out to MacIntyre.

■   ■   ■

The news media gave equal attention to the ever-increasing natural disasters and strange experiences being reported, such as pulsating multicolored lights in the Everglades just as the hurricane hit. More and more rumors circulated that fed on one another, somehow linking with the televised story of a young girl visited by what she had called "a fairy." Her story had gone viral, in the wake of yet another recent disaster, to conclude that aliens were there, disrupting nature and attempting to corrupt the young, even to possibly control their minds.

■   ■   ■

As police and medical first responders, Gary and Nina Goodsen had comprehensive plans in place for their family's security in the event of a disaster. Their central Florida home was well constructed of concrete block and Gary had installed operable shutters. The family had gone outside and secured any objects that could be picked up by high winds. Blowing objects from outside could break not only their own, but any uncovered neighbor's windows, letting in wind and driving rain. The pressure could lift off the roof.

They had a "hurricane kit" supplied with essentials such as flashlights, fresh batteries, and first aid supplies. The NOAA weather radio was always on with backup batteries installed. They kept a stock of bottled water and nonperishable food that didn't need to be cooked. Although hurricanes were rare in the center of the state where they were located, they were not unknown; lesser storms from severe thunderstorms to named tropical storms were frequent. The family knew what to do.

Now their plans had to be hastily implemented as the rogue storm turned north, poised to slice through the center of the state, aimed right for their locale.

The hurricane cut a swath of destruction for most of the day, and by late afternoon Gary was called to emergency duty. Left in charge, Nina checked and rechecked preparations. Liam was tied, as usual, to the umbilical cord of his tablet's headphones. Emma was cranky and unable to focus on any of her favorite indoor activities, complaining of a headache that worsened as the storm approached.

Hurricanes took their time, announcing themselves first with intermittent bands of rain and wind. Thunder and lightning weren't always components, but suddenly formed tornadoes could be. For those in its path, a hurricane demanded patience. The experience could range from simple boredom and "cabin fever" from being imprisoned within boarded-up windows, to the likelihood of a power outage lasting from hours to days, to severe damage, injury, and death. For the Goodsens, who were far enough away from a coast to avoid deadly storm surges, this storm was mainly a torrential rain and wind event. As it worsened, even Liam joined Nina and Emma to huddle together on the floor in front of a sofa, as rain pounded the roof, and wind whistled and roared. The house heaved and groaned as they felt wind whipping against every surface with such force they feared the structure would crumble around them. A loud crack reverberated and the power went out. With the windows shuttered, the house was in darkness.

"Should I light the battery lanterns?" Liam rose.

"No, save them," Nina replied. "We can just use the flashlights until we want to prepare some food later."

"Okay. Good plan." Liam moved toward the dining room where they had placed their storm provisions, some on and some under the table.

"My head hurts!" Emma shrieked. She rolled on the floor grasping her head in both hands, tears rolling down her cheeks.

Nina tried to gather the child in her arms, but Emma squirmed and began running. She banged into Liam as he returned. He dropped the flashlights and grabbed her. "What's wrong, kiddo?" He squatted to be face to face with her.

"It's screaming at me to make them stop. But I don't know who I'm supposed to make stop what!" She bawled.

"Who is screaming at you?" Liam held her shoulders and locked eyes with her.

"The storm!"

"What does its voice sound like?" He held onto her, forcing her to maintain eye contact.

"Not a voice; it's just yelling in my head." She wrenched free of his grasp and clasped her hands over her ears.

Nina watched the exchange with growing alarm. Emma was young and extremely sensitive; she hadn't anticipated the trauma this storm could inflict on her daughter. Liam was often the only family member who could reach Emma when she was in a tumultuous emotional state. Nina decided to stay out of it a few more minutes to give Liam a chance to calm the child.

"How can it yell without a voice?" Liam sat on the floor watching his sister intently. She ignored his question, hands still covering her ears.

He looked at Nina questioningly. She slowly approached Emma from behind and gently put her arms around the girl, "It's all right, sweetie," she murmured. "This bad ole storm is yelling at all of us. We hear that wind howling and rain beating down too."

Emma dropped her arms and turned to face her mother. She shook her head. "It says my name. Keeps saying I can make them stop. But I don't know who they are or what they need to stop!" Tears flowed down her face. She put her arms around Nina and burrowed into her.

"It won't last a lot longer, sweetie. Hey, I'm getting kinda hungry. How about you? Let's go make some peanut butter and jelly sandwiches."

Liam grinned. "Great idea. One good thing about this storm. Peanut butter and jelly for dinner!"

Emma was much calmer. She stood back from Nina and turned to face Liam. "Is it aliens?"

Liam swallowed loudly. "Aw, I don't think so." He looked at Nina as if to say he wasn't totally convinced of what he was saying.

CHAPTER FIVE

The day turned raw and gray, clouds hanging so low Jeff felt he could reach up and touch them. They trudged farther into the wilderness in silence.

"Do you need to wait for night to try to make the contact?" he asked his companions.

"Not necessarily," Annilu replied. "We do need seclusion, though."

Within an expanse of tall, thin trees, moss-covered rocks, logs and fallen tree trunks, huge orange mushrooms broke the dark forest palette. They followed a narrow, winding trail. Jeff's boots made no sound as he stepped through the detritus, remnants of leaves, rock, and the myriad components of a complex ecosystem. Jeff breathed in the distinct forest aroma. A sense of peace and contentment settled within him.

"That looks interesting." Judilay pointed to a rocky overhang ahead. It formed a canopy over what looked like a shallow cave. "Let's explore." The two Synons moved into the shadows. Jeff instinctively hung back. If this was a good spot to talk to Mother Earth he'd stay out of the way.

They returned quickly. "Not really a cave," Judilay said. "But maybe we'll find one if we keep on this trail."

Jeff nodded. "There are many caves. Some Cherokee hid in them in the nineteenth century when the federal government forced them to abruptly abandon their homes here and walk to Oklahoma. Many died. It's called the Trail of Tears. Those who hid formed the remaining Eastern Band that now lives on the Qualla Boundary and the town named Cherokee."

"We need to learn more about that," Judilay said soberly. "I hope we can visit Cherokee."

"It's not far from here. I hope you can visit. The museum immerses you in history, and you can experience it at a recreated village and an outdoor drama."

They had resumed their trek. Jeff fell back into contentment edged with a tingle of anticipation, aware of their mission. His mind snapped back to its routine program. It was hard to tell the time in the darkened forest. Jeff glanced at his watch and saw that it was approaching noon. "Let's look for a spot to sit a minute so I can grab some food and water. I really wish I could siphon energy from my surroundings like you two."

They both looked at him with chagrin. "We don't siphon energy," Annilu snapped.

Jeff affected an exaggerated wince. "Ooh, sorry for using the wrong word."

Before the conversation could go further a loud buzz came from Jeff's shoulder bag. He took out a device and pulled up an antenna on it. "Satellite phone," he explained as he connected. "Jeff Hawke here."

"Jeff. It's Lew. A hurricane crossed the Everglades and is moving up the center of Florida. Its projected path brings it right through here by tomorrow. You need to abort the mission and head back."

Jeff was so stunned that he just stood staring at the phone for a moment. "Hurricane? Hit Everglades and is coming here?" His skin felt like something was slithering over it. "Have you heard from Tork?"

"No."

"Is She after us??"

"This is a sat phone, Jeff. Not totally secure. We'll talk when you get back."

Jeff shut down the phone and put it away. His companions were silent.

"I guess you heard some of that." They nodded. "We have to get back as quickly as we can. A bad storm is coming by tomorrow. Man, it's about noon now. We can't get out of here before dark."

"Jeff, we can get you out right away," Annilu said.

Something like panic swept over him as he realized what she meant. "Oh no! I'm organic, you know."

Judilay chuckled. "So was the material our clothing is made from. "Do you meditate?"

"Meditate? I guess I do a little."

"You are Native American?"

"Yeah."

"Did you have any training that involved a trance? Not drug induced."

"No. Indians don't have magic. They have spiritual ceremonies. As a teen I participated in a sweat lodge. I don't know that I went into what you'd call a trance, but it might have been close. I remember my buddies giggling. They sounded far off, not part of where I was."

Jeff suddenly remembered the crisis in which renegade Synons had control of his city's computer network and TuMa'Aye Gra'Vay entered the system in her natural form, linked to his psyche as he sat at a computer terminal. He had been in an altered state of consciousness. "Your queen somehow linked to my mind once, and I was in a total trance."

"Let's go back to that overhang," Annilu said, turning and stalking back down the trail.

Judilay motioned Jeff to follow. When they reached the spot, Jeff was invited to join the two Synons in the deepest recess of the cave-like area. It was dark and smelled of dampness and decaying matter. The two Synons asked him to be totally still and silent. They closed their eyes and felt along the rocky wall. Should he close his eyes too? They didn't tell him to, and curiosity compelled him to watch them. After what seemed an interminable time, they turned back to him. "There is a Passageway here," Annilu stated.

"A Passageway? Isn't that like a black hole?" Jeff felt panic rising again. What were they thinking?

"Not exactly." Judilay grinned.

"Jeff, close your eyes and clear your mind. Do whatever mental exercises you can to totally relax and not think. Reach for the trance state you know you can achieve. You are part of Nature. You are not separate from Nature." Annilu began to chant at him. "You are one with Nature and The Living World." Judilay's voice joined in. Jeff concentrated on listening to the chants. He figured it was a form of hypnosis. He hoped he'd black out soon—and wake up somewhere else. He didn't exactly black out. He was aware, but it was dreamlike. He wasn't a body. He just existed. He felt gentle touches. He was being guided. He felt like light going through a prism. He burst forth in all the colors of the rainbow.

       ■   ■   ■

Jeff looked down. He was standing on solid ground, but felt woozy. Fragments of memory hovered like dream images. Jeff looked around and saw Judilay and Annilu on either side of him, concern on their faces. "Are you all right?" Judilay said, gently taking Jeff's arm.

The memory solidified; Jeff whooped. "Never thought I'd get beamed up!" He giggled, staggering. Annilu and Judilay grabbed him by his arms and dragged him down the path from the Passageway from which they had exited to their vehicle. Jeff continued mumbling, "No, not beamed up. And not down. Over?" He slumped. The Synons gently shoved him into the back seat of the car. He lay there, mumbling.

"Do you know how to work this mechanism?" Annilu asked Judilay, who sat in the driver's seat looking a bit bewildered. Both ignored Jeff's mumbling.

Judilay admitted, "I did drive a vehicle on a prior visit, but it was not like this one. Let me meditate a moment."

Annilu turned to Jeff, who was lying on the back seat with one arm over his eyes, still mumbling. "Jeff, can you pull yourself together and get us back to the facility?" He just kept mumbling. "Jeff! Sit up and look at me!" She used a form of voice that carried a hint of command.

Jeff bolted upright. "Whaa...?"

"Get your head straight!"

Judilay, looking sheepish, got out of the vehicle and opened the back door. "Jeff, do you have the ignition key?"

"Key? Oh yeah. It's in the zipper compartment inside my bag." He just sat there.

"You still have the bag crossed over your head. Can you get the key out, please?"

"Oh, sure." He fumbled with the outer zipper, then the inner one, and held up the keys. "Here you go."

"Uh, do you think you're able to drive us back?" Judilay took the dangling keys.

"Back? Where?"

"I hope this isn't going to be permanent." Judilay gave Annilu a worried look. "I know of no human ever being taken though a Passageway before. I don't know what the aftereffects can be."

"He's not like other humans." Annilu stated flatly. "But he might be in shock. I recall observing that in humans who had traumatic experiences. Perhaps making him do normal things will help. Jeff." The commanding voice returned. "Get in the driver's seat and take us back to the facility. Now."

"Okay. No need to get huffy about it." He complied.

Judilay reached over and put the key into the ignition. "Now start it."

Jeff sat a moment, still looking dazed, then turned the ignition, put the vehicle in reverse, and backed out of the parking spot. "Can I tell the others what we did?" He grinned impishly.

"No!" both Synons exploded.

"Well, in confidence, maybe Henderson and MacIntyre." Judilay met Jeff's impish grin with an impish grin.

■   ■   ■

Annilu had been right. Being forced to do a common action cleared Jeff's head. Driving was an automatic habit and he drove toward the facility without thinking about it. As they drove, all three were silent, which Jeff was glad of. His thoughts were logically ordering themselves. He surveyed recent events in an almost clinical fashion. Awe swept over him. He had traveled through one Passageway to another and come out in one piece. It must really have been like the *Star Trek* transporter. Molecules—or atoms?—broken down, transported through space, and reassembled at a separate location in the original package. Had other people done this?

The Synons' recent conversation about him floated in his memory like the remnant of a dream. He had been lying on the back seat, feeling disoriented, like he had just come out of anesthesia. They had never done this with a person before! Then Annilu's voice was in his head stating that he "wasn't like other people." What did she mean by that? He could understand having some kind of psychic ability. TuMa'Aye Gra'Vay had told him she was certain he could telepathically communicate with Synons. That he could sort of see. Thoughts could be a form of energy that could transcend physical barriers.

His body was flesh and bone and blood like other people. How was he so different that he could be disassembled and reassembled? His material body would have transformed into energy that could travel through a Passageway and then reform his physical body. Were these Synons that powerful? The Synons had explained that their true nature was a form of energy-mind-spirit that made it logical that they could easily traverse Passageways. They could transform their energy into matter once on Earth. Bodies did that with food, transforming it into fuel to power the body and renew cells. Maybe people could do what Synons did but hadn't yet figured it out. At any rate, these Synons were able to take him through two Passageways. But how could he be sure they had reformed him exactly as he had been?

■ ■ ■

When they got back to the facility, the storm was attacking with heavy wind and rain. Only a skeleton crew was on duty. Not surprisingly, Lew Henderson and MacIntyre met them at the door and ushered them into the secure conference room.

"What the hell did you do?" MacIntyre attacked Annilu and Judilay as soon as they were seated. The two looked like children caught disobeying their parents. If, as Jeff had been told, they had no emotions, their human personas were doing a fine job of fabricating terrified, guilty expressions. He felt bad for them.

Jeff jumped into the silence. "They did the only thing that could save me."

"You can't be sure of that." Henderson's calm tone soothed the atmosphere a bit.

Annilu found her composure. "Your communication was a clear command. Get Jeff out of the way of a dangerous approaching storm. Had we begun walking back to the vehicle, even at the fastest pace he could manage, the storm would have overtaken us on the trail where there was no shelter or protection, in darkness."

"I think Synons should have the resources to meet such a challenge," MacIntyre retorted. "You could have found a way to protect him. Plus, Jeff is a very experienced woodsman and an Air Force veteran. He is well versed in survival tactics. Your action was reckless. The consequences could have been catastrophic."

Henderson looked pensive. "To my knowledge, no Synon has ever accomplished what these two did. It's a major step forward for us. We need to document exactly how they did it."

"That may be. But the risk was far too great. A human life could have been destroyed. Not to mention the loss of our strongest human ally."

Jeff was taken aback by MacIntyre's last remark. He was their strongest human ally? He was speechless and felt himself blushing.

"Oh, Jeff. Get over it." Henderson chuckled. "I've known you a long time and have always been aware of your potential. Just don't let it go to your head." He grinned broadly.

The two guilty Synons had sat quietly during this exchange. Now Annilu stood, posture erect, and declared, "We must return to the Realm and contemplate. And document our action. Those more experienced than us might be able to take our crude methods and refine them into a safe process that could revolutionize our capabilities."

"No!" Judilay jumped up to confront her. "That means that other Synons would be sent here to complete our mission. Our experience here is too valuable to discard. I agree that we should document our method and share it with the Realm. But I am not ready to abandon my mission."

"Has anyone heard from Tork?" Jeff deflected the conversation. "If he succeeded the mission might change."

MacIntyre's bushy eyebrows knitted. "He was unsuccessful."

Jeff gaped at him. "Did he talk to Earth?"

Mac's mouth tightened. "For now, the statement I just made will suffice." His expression soured. "But there are reports all over the south Florida media about strange, pulsating, colored lights in the middle of the Everglades. It's overshadowing the news of the freak storm that hit there. We can surmise that those lights somehow involved Tork."

▪   ▪   ▪

Jeff, Annilu and Judilay were exhausted and frustrated. They had been ordered to "relax" in the break room that contained comfy couches and chairs. They sat forlornly, the two Synons stiffly in chairs, while Jeff sipped a beer, slouched in a recliner. They had turned on only a couple of lamps, keeping most of the room in shadow, which seemed to fit their mood. All had remained silent after their debriefing and scolding. Jeff just wanted to go home to his cozy cabin and cuddle up with Marie and Cosmos. His mind seemed to have uncharacteristically shut down. He wondered vaguely if it were an effect of the experience he'd had or just an inability to process it. The quiet was broken by the creak of the door opening; MacIntyre and Henderson entered. They surveyed the group and exchanged glances; then, as if planned, both sat on a couch next to a floor lamp that threw pale light across them.

Henderson spoke in a calm, quiet tone. "Now that you've had a chance to rest, we need to give you a full report on Tork's telepathed message. He's all right. He succeeded in contacting Earth, but she was very ill and barely communicative. All he got from her was a cryptic 'only they can help.'"

Jeff grunted but said nothing. He stared into his beer as if it would provide the answers he needed. Somehow, it was more difficult to accept the Earth as a living entity that one might talk to than that he had traveled via a "transporter" mode from one location to another.

Judilay asked, "Who does she mean? Humans?"

MacIntyre replied, "She didn't respond to queries about Synons or humans. But who else is there? It seems that she's saying if we want to help we must work through people. Tork is consulting with the Realm on it."

Judilay almost whispered, "If Tork couldn't form a stronger link we would likely have failed. Jeff's life was risked for nothing."

MacIntyre shook his head. "Not for nothing. You were foolhardy, but you did take a major step forward. You need to focus on documenting the experience, especially what actions you took in relating to Jeff."

Jeff grunted again. "Man, I wish I could share it with people."

"Under no circumstances!" MacIntyre boomed. "No talking to anybody. Not Marie, not the crew here. No one other than us and Tork. That's an order of the highest security consideration from an NSA representative directly to you as an American citizen. Can I be any plainer about the gravity of this?" His eyebrows rose like tumbleweed scooped up in a wind.

Jeff nodded, frustration rising in him. "I need to hear you say it," MacIntyre ordered.

"Okay! I won't tell a living human about being transported through Passageways. Can I talk to Cosmos about it? I can sort of talk with him without speaking aloud." He said it mostly in jest and was surprised at the reaction.

"You what?" Henderson jumped up.

"Well, I think I can communicate with my cat telepathically. He stares at me and seems to understand what I say." That was mostly true. Cosmos had touched his mind the first time Jeff had seen him as the cat wound around his legs and announced—without a word—that Tami Graves had said Jeff would take care of him. He recalled picking up the cat and looking into his intelligent green eyes. In that moment they bonded in a way that was different from his soul mate bond with Marie. The ancient concept of totem animals fleeted through his mind, and yet this was not the same.

Annilu's guffaw pulled him out of his reverie. "Does this cat reply directly to you?" she asked skeptically.

"Well, yeah. Sometimes I swear I hear a little voice in my head, agreeing with me or offering advice. You know, Tami Graves found him and sent him to us. Me and Marie."

"We need to run some experiments," MacIntyre stated, no humor evident. "After you provide a detailed, descriptive documentation of your Passageway experience."

"You want me to document what I experienced? It might read like it was written by someone on an acid trip."

Henderson was smiling as he regarded Jeff affectionately. "Just write every detail of what you felt and thought. Please work with us. You are a unique person, young man. You and your cat. But you must not share any of this with Marie."

"I understand about keeping quiet about the Passageways, but Marie knows that Cosmos and I have conversations." He didn't think he could keep things from Marie. Even if he didn't speak about them. She recognized he had a higher security clearance than her and knew things that were forbidden to her, but something as close to them as his relationship with Cosmos would be hard to suppress. Besides, how would he bring Cosmos to the facility for experiments without her knowing about it?

"She knows what she sees and what you tell her. Let's leave it at that. I know you two are close, but we absolutely cannot contaminate an experiment by having any outside communication," MacIntyre asserted. "We'll go over what you can tell her and concoct a story about your expedition. She does have clearance for the primary mission, as do all of your team here, but these new developments go beyond what we can share with them."

Jeff looked more forlorn than before. He sighed deeply and ran a hand through his hair. Of course they would figure out a way to prevent Marie from knowing they were experimenting on Cosmos. "I understand and will comply," he muttered. But I can't speak for my cat, he said to himself.

CHAPTER SIX

The little girl, Emma, always lay nestled in the back of Tork's mind. Now that his attention was no longer consumed by the need to focus solely on what was happening in the moment, he could explore what was undoubtedly a unique mind closely connected to The Living World and open to Synon communication. Instead of going directly to the Realm, he decided to stop off in central Florida. He needed to accomplish his goal without causing trauma to Emma or creating the kind of incident that Annilu had inadvertently triggered when she improvised and used the child's openness to The Living World as a Passageway. The ensuing publicity was still floating around social media. He toyed with the idea of reaching Emma while she slept. If she, by any chance, was aware of his mental presence and talked about it, adults would dismiss it as simply more fanciful dreams.

He thought about the girl's insistence that both he and Annilu were fairies. Emma obviously had some intrinsic awareness of her ability to mentally communicate with them. The notion of fairies frequently appeared in children's entertainment and story books. In fact, fairies represented archetypical beings that had appeared around the Earth for most of humanity's existence, in folklore, mythology, and literature, assuming many forms, sizes, personalities, and magical abilities. Many actual sightings of what people thought were fairies and similar fanciful creatures had actually been Synons. They often chose a persona in the form of such otherworldly entities from the culture in which they were presently attempting to communicate with people, or implement an action. Tork chuckled. Now it seemed that the "otherworldly" entities of lore were extraterrestrials. Even Emma Goodsen's twelve-year-old brother had insisted that she had seen an alien, not a fairy. But a five-year-old like her would more readily relate to a being from the story books, movies, and theme park visits that comprised her fantasy world. He could cloak his mental intrusion by presenting it as a dream in which a fairy visited her.

Emma's open mind was a beacon directing Tork directly to the Goodsen home. In a human persona, he strolled the community of neat concrete block homes clad in stucco and painted in pale pastels. The neighborhood was out in full force cleaning up storm debris. Huge oak limbs and uprooted pine trees littered yards and sidewalks. A couple of trees had fallen on homes. FEMA personnel were putting blue tarpaulins on damaged roofs even while workers were beginning to repair or replace others. The yards were lushly landscaped, and a few vivid blossoms bravely smiled from drenched and mangled vegetation. It was easy for Tork to blend in with the activity, but he couldn't linger and risk being noticed. He walked out of the residential area of the Goodsen home and found a park nestled around a small lake where he sat on a bench. Cleanup work was underway in the park, but no one paid any attention to the elderly man sitting on a bench feeding ducks.

There was ample vegetation in which to hide and transform once night fell and the park emptied of people. The elderly man strolled along the sidewalks and stopped at a hedge around some picnic tables. If someone had seen what he did next it would have been a comical and incongruous sight. He crawled into the hedge. After some time, a colorful light show emanated from it. Its branches parted slightly and a wisp of breeze with a faint glow emerged.

Power had been restored to the Goodsens' street. The home was dark except for several exterior lights. Emma's sleeping mind drew him to her. Tork's focused energy easily traversed the double-paned window of her room, and he hovered over the child. Rather than peaceful slumber, he discovered a psyche in turmoil.

■　　■　　■

Emma was in no particular place. Haze hung around her. The Voice had lost its force. It was faint, but insistent. "You must make them stop. You must make them stop." She ran, but the Voice was still there. She covered her ears, but the Voice persisted in her head. She could not get away from it. Then she was aware of a new presence. The haze took on a glow of color. Calm enveloped her. A new voice soothed her. "Don't fear the message. The Earth needs your help. You love the Earth, don't you?"

"Uh huh."

"It is her Voice you hear, asking you for help. Don't fear that Voice. You can save her. I will help you do what you need to. You will not be alone."

"Are you the fairy who visited me before?"

"A different one. There are many of us who protect you."

"What am I supposed to do? I'm only five years old."

"You are a wise five-year-old. You should tell everyone how much the Earth needs them to take care of her. She is very sick. People have made her sick. People have to stop abusing her so that she can get well."

"I tell Mommy and Daddy? And my brother?"

"Yes. And everybody else you see. At Sunday school, in kindergarten, in the playground. Your neighbors and relatives. Most important, ask them to tell everyone they see the same thing. It must spread."

"What will happen to me if Earth dies?"

"We won't let that happen."

* * *

Tork was convinced that there were other children like Emma. Perhaps a leap in evolution was occurring. If Earth could survive long enough for Emma's generation to grow up, perhaps human attitudes and actions would change. It seemed a long time in human terms, but not so long in the lifetime of Earth and the Realm. But conditions were worsening at a rapid pace. The Realm needed to put to work as many Synons as possible to intervene in any way they could, while maintaining their secrecy. It was time to again enlist the help of those many Synons who had made their homes on Earth living as humans. More than ever they needed to be united. He would go to the Realm to make a report and plan with TuMa'Aye Gra'vay.

* * *

Emma talked and talked about how a fairy had told her she needed to tell everybody to start being nice to the Earth. At first, the adults smiled and shook their heads. Kids and their imaginations!

When she persisted during the late summer kindergarten classes, she was scolded and burst into tears. "But the Earth told me to tell everybody."

"Well, you've told us," her teacher replied sarcastically. "We heard you the first time. Now be quiet and pay attention to the lesson."

The response in Sunday school was a bit harsher. "Emma, fairies are fun, but they are made up. They don't exist."

Once again, Emma's tears came as she tried to explain. "It's not just the fairy that talked to me. He told me the Voice I was hearing was the Earth."

"Now hush, Emma! The Earth can't talk. If you want to talk about something, speak to Jesus. He'll listen to you."

In a small but resilient voice Emma answered, "Okay. I'll ask Jesus to help the Earth."

"That's nice, Emma."

Liam had a different take. He was the big brother. The protector. He displayed patience uncharacteristic of a twelve-year-old boy. He gently questioned Emma about her dream. Her answers were consistent. She was unwavering in her determination. He grew uneasy.

■　■　■

Emma was successful. She told a lot of people, none of whom took it seriously. Then, an older child at the school playground pointed her smartphone at Emma and asked her to repeat her story for the camera so that she could pass it on to many, many people. Emma was thrilled. The girl posted it on social media in public mode, and, just as she had promised, Emma's message reached many, many people.

■　■　■

Jeff knew that the order to get him out of the high forest before the storm hit had been a sound one. His two Synon companions had taken the only possible route to get him safely out of harm's way, albeit into a potentially disastrous situation, despite their confidence that he could be safely taken through Passageways. But he had many questions.

The next day Jeff sought out Baily MacIntyre, who was huddling with Annilu and Judilay. "Mac, I need to talk to you a minute."

Mac looked at him quizzically. "Sure, Jeff. Let's take a walk down by the water." He turned to the two Synons. "You know how to proceed. We'll catch up later."

The two strolled in silence until they had exited the building and were walking along the bulkhead to sit on a bench watching as the sun rippled on the rushing water.

Mac waited for Jeff to speak.

Jeff felt emboldened, almost entitled to have his questions answered. "Does the President know what you are?" he blurted.

Mac chuckled. "Of course not. Presidents change every four to eight years. Some could handle the knowledge, others couldn't, and some might seek to use the knowledge for personal gain. Besides, we need them to remain—"

"Clueless. So that you can manipulate them."

Mac looked hurt. "That's never our intention, Jeff. Please believe me. I know you feel used, but our very existence is mandated to serve humanity."

"What proof can you show me of that?"

Mac stopped and gaped at him. "Jeff, what's going on with you? We've been through a lot together. It never occurred to me that you had any doubts about us."

Jeff's fists clenched along with his teeth. "I think you had me under some kind of cloaking spell to keep me from questioning you. Now that spell is broken; my analytical abilities are back. You showed me a magic show. How you can change shapes. I saw evil invade our cyber network and you flushed him out. But it turned out he was one of you anyway. More shapeshifting shows. Then I learn there are a bunch of you living here masquerading as people. I see no evidence of where you really come from or what your ultimate goal is. You could just as easily be from another planet and infiltrating us for your own benefit. Maybe—"

"Jeff!" Mac's voice had a tinge of command to it. "You sound like a bad science fiction movie, or one of those crazy conspiracy people. We need your focused intellect." He paused, gazing into the water. "I don't know how to give you proof. You went through two small Passageways relatively close to each other. On Earth. I don't think we can physically take you to the Realm. It couldn't sustain your biological integrity."

Jeff stared at Mac with a stunned expression. "You'd consider taking me to the Realm?"

"If I could. But, of course, you might just assume I had taken you to another planet within this universe."

Jeff looked touched, then his countenance changed abruptly to his signature scowl.

"Sure. You'd take me to the Realm if it were possible. But since it's not possible, oh well. Too bad. No proof. I just have to take your word for it." He considered a moment. "Haven't others had this same skepticism? Seems like quite a few of us know about you."

"Far fewer than you think. It's quite unusual that your entire team here has been told about us. Many others with security clearance above theirs don't know. But your team is bright in an unusual way. Not just technical. You're open-minded and visionary. That's why you were all selected. But you are the only one who seems to have genuinely unique qualities that connect you to us."

"Me and my cat."

Mac laughed out loud, in a very human way. "You and your cat. Yes. By the way, why don't you invite me and Lew over for dinner one night."

"But you don't really need food. Seems a waste."

"We use the food for fuel the same as you; our process is just different. Or, we could drop by for a drink one evening to enjoy the ambience of your home."

"And secretly test my cat."

"We don't need to test him. We have telepathy with animals."

"So you can just ask him if I'm telepathic with him."

"We could do that. Better to witness it, however."

"You really do believe this, huh? That I'm telepathic, at least with my cat?"

"You're the one who said it." Mac grinned. "Look, Jeff. You'll learn more as time goes on. I just know that we need you. The Earth needs you."

■　■　■

The Tech Center plodded on, processing the continuous stream of data from the young Josh Jackson, formerly Bandela. The team caught up with routine maintenance. There was a sense of the surreal, accented by their physical isolation. They were the only few humans on Earth aware of the crisis the planet was enduring. An uncharted island.

Jeff tried to act normal, overseeing small projects that had been set aside. None of his team was aware of his extraordinary experience. They just knew that the impending storm had forced him and the two Synons to abandon the attempt to contact Earth. That was hard enough to process. Midafternoon, after consulting with Mac, Jeff told the team to knock off early and get some relaxation away from the facility. He invited Lew and Mac to stop by and told Marie while they were driving home together. "We can all benefit from just sitting by the creek a while," he told her. "They need their Nature fix more than we do, you know." He grinned. Marie knew about the Synon mission, but not, of course, how he had left the forest. She had not questioned him, knowing that he would tell her what he could. She grinned back at him. "I'll fix some iced tea for them to pretend to drink."

Lew and Mac perked up in the bucolic environment that was Jeff and Marie's yard. Marie brought the tea and disappeared back into the house, Cosmos traipsing along behind her. Lew nudged Jeff. "Call the cat back," he whispered.

Jeff said nothing, just looking at the cat. Cosmos stopped, turned, cocked his head, watching Jeff, then ambled back toward him.

"You did it?" Lew grinned. Mac looked astounded.

Jeff smirked.

"Did you call him telepathically, or did you use some kind of signal that he understands?" Mac growled.

Jeff continued to smirk. "He was facing away from me. He couldn't have seen a signal. Did you hear me make any sounds?" The two visitors shook their heads.

"How did you do it? Is there a special way you reach out to him?" Lew leaned forward to pet the black head that was rubbing against his leg.

"I said his name in my mind but was also looking at him and picturing him walking back to me. Then I said to him in my mind come back to me. He did." A big grin split Jeff's face.

"Does he talk back to you?"

"Of course not. He can't speak English. I get impressions from him. Not words. We just understand each other."

Mac rubbed his chin, watching the cat. "We need to do brain scans while they are communicating."

"Oh no." Jeff waved his arms as he shook his head vigorously. "You aren't putting my cat through being hooked up to machines. I mean, how can you even make a cat be still? And if you sedate him how can he communicate?"

Mac was insistent. "A monitor like they use in hospitals. Minimal attachment. We can give him a light sedative. You can be holding him all the time. We can make it work."

"What do we tell Marie?"

Mac and Lew looked at each other; Mac nodded. "Yeah, we can have her take the two Synons on a field trip somewhere. A fun day trip for them all. They wanted to see more of the area around here."

Jeff picked up Cosmos who curled up in his lap. "Okay, boy. We're going to be guinea pigs."

* * *

With Mac's connections, it only took a day for the necessary equipment to arrive. Marie, Annilu, and Judilay were glad to be told to take a day off. The storm had been intense but swift and now the skies were blue and clear. It would be good to get out. Marie was a bit shy about being "in charge" of the two alien beings for an entire day, but their eagerness and the time they spent researching and planning it developed a comfortable ease among them.

The tests went smoothly. Cosmos, slightly sedated, cuddled on a bed next to Jeff, purring. Jeff soothed the cat with soft sounds and caresses, mentally telling him that no one would hurt him. He even explained the nature of the activity to his pet. Maybe Cosmos would understand.

When Jeff got home, it was so late that Marie was already asleep. He tried not to wake her. He wasn't sure he could face the questions he was pledged not to answer. He lay next to her, grateful for the familiarity of her presence and the comfort of their home. Cosmos slept curled in the crook of her arm. He momentarily glanced at Jeff, then was asleep again.

Exhaustion claimed Jeff's body, but his mind felt more alert than it had in a long time. Instead of drifting off to the mental escape of sleep, Jeff felt like he was emerging from a haze that had cloaked his natural curiosity about the Synons. He marveled at how he had so easily accepted but seldom questioned them. Despite Mac's denial, he decided that they had deliberately muddled his mind. That thought touched a nerve and memories of how TuMa'Aye Gra'Vay had plundered his mind to fashion herself as "the woman of his dreams, Tami Graves." Resentment seethed. He felt used, taken advantage of, his innermost-self invaded. He had struggled with this, yet was still unable to accept her explanation that she selected him because he was "special" and she knew he was the human they needed at that time. He supposed he should be flattered, but the underlying premise that Synons could intrude into the one area of individual privacy most sacred to people was unsettling and a bit terrifying. His mind whirled. Did they want to train him to be like them, rooting around in people's minds for useful information? He shuddered.

What if he did have that ability? The Synons believed that was why they had been able to take him through Passageways. They kept telling him he was special. Even his long-time friend, Lewis Henderson. Lew. All those years Jeff never had the slightest inkling that he was anything other than a wise old Cherokee running a cultural center. In some ways, it was like science fiction with alien beings living among and impersonating humans. The humans never knew who to trust. Who was who? But these Synons insisted they were not hostile aliens intent on taking over the human race. Their mission was to help humans. They were emissaries from The Living World. If anything, they were like guardian angels. Their presence should be reassuring. His mind raced on. What if they were lying? Why did he just believe them? Warm fur touched his shoulder. The rhythmic music of purring was palpable. A damp, rough tongue ever so lightly grazed his ear. Cosmos settled next to Jeff's head. The tumult of thought receded and Jeff's mind relaxed like a soothing balm had enveloped it.

CHAPTER SEVEN

It was still summer and school was out, but Emma continued to attend kindergarten. Emma liked it. They had many activities outside in the playground, especially in the morning before the heat of the day brought thunderstorms. A new girl named Sandy arrived, and soon her mother, Mrs. Johnson, volunteered as a teaching assistant. She brought with her books about fairies that Emma had not seen. In the afternoons, when they had quiet reading time, Emma and Sandy would huddle together and look at them, then make up their own stories of what happened to the characters after the books ended. It only took a couple of weeks for them to become good friends.

One rainy afternoon, when they were reading a new book Emma whispered to Sandy, "Can I tell you a secret?"

Sandy's eyes widened, "Sure!"

"Promise you won't tell anyone?"

"Okay. Promise."

"I've seen actual fairies. They talked to me."

"Oh!!" Sandy's blue eyes were as round as the pink mouth that formed the excited sound.

"In our car. There was an earthquake, and Mommy and Daddy went to help other people. Liam was asleep. Then a fairy talked to me in my head."

"Was it a girl or boy fairy?"

"A girl. I saw her just for a minute, and then she disappeared."

"What did she say?"

"She said they would help us."

"The fairies will help us? How? What for?"

"I don't know. But then I saw a man that I knew was a fairy. I tried to talk to him but my daddy took me away."

"A man? Like a regular person? I didn't know fairies looked like men."

"Me neither. But I knew he was a fairy. Then one night a fairy talked to me in my dreams. He told me to tell everyone to stop hurting the Earth."

"Hurting the Earth? What does that mean?"

"I'm not sure. But he told me to tell everybody I know."

■　　■　　■

Emma's mother and Mrs. Johnson met at a parents' open house. Nina Goodsen was glad that her daughter, who was more out-going in the company of adults than children, had apparently bonded with her first "best friend." Heather Johnson's husband was in the military, deployed overseas, so she and Sandy were staying with Mrs. Johnson's family. Nina warmed to Heather and invited her and Sandy to the Goodsen home for a Sunday afternoon cookout. Gary was all too happy to support military families and welcomed them, but he spent little time conversing with Heather as the two women were busy exchanging tales of mothering preschool girls. When they sat down to eat, he asked a few friendly questions about her family and how she was adjusting to life there. Heather's husband was in the Middle East and she was concerned about him. The Goodsens felt sympathy for the Johnson family.

A few days later Heather called Nina near the end of the school day at the hospital where she worked. "Hi, Nina, got a minute?"

"Yes, I can talk. I have desk duty right now."

"Sandy told Emma about her storybook doll collection and Emma is begging to see it. Could I take her over to our place after school for a while, then drop her off at home before your dinner time?"

Nina hesitated. She had not been to the Johnson home, but she knew that they lived with Heather's retired parents. Gary was careful about where the kids, especially Emma at her age, went without one of them. But Heather was a friend, and Nina was glad that Sandy's friendship seemed to have brought Emma out of her shell. She knew Emma would be disappointed if she wasn't allowed to visit Sandy.

"Nina? Are you still there?"

"Oh, yes. I was just distracted a moment. Sure. Emma can go home with you. Would you like one of us to pick her up in a little while? I get off in about an hour."

"I have a church meeting at four o'clock, and it'll be easy for me to drop Emma off on my way. I know you need to get your family's dinner started."

"Thank you. It is my night to cook. I'll look for you a little before four then."

"Great! Be prepared for Emma to talk nonstop. She is so lively and adorable."

Nina laughed. It was so wonderful to hear her withdrawn little girl described that way. "Thanks. See you later."

* * *

Four o'clock arrived but brought no Emma. Nina called Heather and got a "number not in service" message. She couldn't find a number in her phone contacts for Heather's parents. She frantically tore into the basket holding scraps of paper on the kitchen counter where her family saved bits of information. Nothing. She called Heather again. Same recording. Nina looked at the clock. The school would be closed by now. No way to check on Heather's home address. After an online search, Nina was beginning to panic. She dug out the paper phone book, which was several years old, but realized she didn't know Heather's maiden name. She lived with her parents, so the home number would not be under Johnson. Just in case Heather had a home phone under her own name, Nina searched the phone book. It was divided up among Orlando and several small cities clustered around it. Heather could live in any one of them. Hoping to hear the doorbell at any moment, she checked every Johnson listing but found no Heather, not even an "H. Johnson." She realized that she and Heather had never exchanged email addresses either. It was nearly five. Gary would be home soon. Liam was in his room. Nina's heart was racing; she felt dizzy. Calm down, she told herself. Heather might be caught in a traffic jam with a mobile phone that needs charging. Wait a while. Prepare dinner.

Nina went through the motions of making a salad. Beyond that her only thought of food was a vague notion of ordering pizza.

Liam's croaky adolescent voice rang out as he loped into the kitchen. "What's for dinner tonight? I don't smell anything." He stopped and stared at his mother. She stood over a salad bowl, tears running down her cheeks. "Mom! What's wrong?"

Nina just stood there. "I think something awful might have happened." It was a whisper.

Liam's first thoughts went to his father. Each time he left for work Gary's family knew they might never see him alive again. "No!" he wailed. "Dad!"

Nina shook her head. "Not Dad."

As if on cue, they heard Gary's car pulling into the garage, the motor shutting down, the door opening and closing.

"He'll be furious with me." Nina sank into a chair burying her face in her hands.

"I'm hooomme!" Gary's ritual greeting rang out as he entered the laundry-mud room, continuing with his ritual by removing his sidearm and shoving it into a lock box in a cabinet. He walked into the kitchen and halted in his tracks. "What's going on?" He went to Nina, trying to put his arms around her. She shrugged away.

"You'll hate me forever." she said in a flat voice.

Gary looked to Liam for an answer but his son only shook his head in bewilderment.

Gary sat in a chair next to Nina and motioned for Liam to sit. He instinctively knew that something was very wrong.

"I could never hate you," he said softly. "Tell me what's wrong."

Liam suddenly sat erect, looking around. "Where's Emma?"

"She's gone!" Nina shouted, jumping up, her chair clattering to the floor. "I stupidly, stupidly…"

Gary leapt up and grabbed her. "Nina, calm down. Tell us what happened."

"Heather. Heather has her."

Gary relaxed a bit. "She's with Heather and Sandy? Why are you so upset?"

Nina's words were gulps now, interspersed with sobs. "She called and asked me to let her take Emma to her home to see Sandy's toys. I was at work, distracted." Her voice rose. "But that's no excuse. I didn't even have her address or another phone number. I didn't know where I was letting my child go!" She sank to her knees, sobbing loudly.

Gary grabbed Nina's phone from the counter, checked the contacts and called Heather's number. A robotic voice announced, "This number is no longer in service." Gary threw the phone down and pulled out his own, punching numbers. "This is Detective Gary Goodsen. I need an immediate Amber Alert issued."

■   ■   ■

Emma awoke feeling groggy. She sat up and saw that she was not in her bed. She was in a strange place. "Mommy? Daddy? Liam?" She got up from what she realized was a couch, but staggered. She looked around. "Mommy! Daddy! Liam! Where are you?" she wailed, bursting into tears, plopping onto the floor in a seated position. A familiar woman entered. "Mrs. Johnson, where am I?" Emma peered up at the woman who approached and drew her to her feet.

"You're on a secret trip, Emma. Come with me to breakfast." Mrs. Johnson led her out the door and down a hallway to a wide metal door with no handle. She pressed a button and the door opened in the center, the two sides sliding back. "Go on in," she pushed Emma gently into what looked like a tall box. Emma balked. It was scary. "Haven't you ever been in an elevator, Emma?" Emma shook her head. "This will be fun." The doors closed and Mrs. Johnson pressed a button. "You'll feel us moving. Then we'll be on the first floor. You slept on the third floor."

"Where are we?" Emma had calmed down a bit in the familiar company.

"I told you. A secret place. We're playing a game." The door opened onto another wide hallway. Heather Johnson pulled Emma out and down the hall, which was lined with tall windows with a view of water.

"We're at the beach!" Emma exclaimed.

"Yes." Heather dragged her into a bright room with a big bay window looking out on the sea. In front of it was a round, glass-topped table and chairs. "You just sit here and your breakfast will be right along."

"Who will eat breakfast with me?"

"Today you get to eat by yourself." Heather briskly walked off into another room.

A dark-skinned lady in a black dress and white apron appeared carrying a tray, which she sat in front of Emma. "Hello there. I'm Luisa," she said. She talked the way some of the children at Emma's school sounded, with an accent. "What's your name?"

"Emma."

"Emma, I brought you a nice breakfast. Now you just sit here and enjoy it. But don't go anywhere until someone comes for you. This is a big house, and you can get lost."

"Thank you," Emma said. Luisa left and Emma looked at the tray of food. It was like her family had on Saturday morning. Scrambled eggs, bacon, grits, and orange juice. Emma was hungry, so she ate.

After she had eaten Emma really needed to go to the bathroom. She squirmed in the chair, hoping someone would come along soon. No one came. She was afraid she might wet her pants. She still wore the clothes she had on at Sandy's house. Emma called out, "Hello, Miss Loosa?" mispronouncing Luisa. "Mrs. Johnson? Where's the bathroom?"

Luisa appeared, smiling kindly. "Come on, I'll take you." She reached for Emma's hand.

They walked back to and along the long hallway. "I saw Mrs. Johnson here, so where is my friend Sandy?" Emma asked.

"Mrs. Johnson? I don't know anybody here by that name, or a Sandy."

■　■　■

Several days after the storm, an early morning meeting was called at the Tech Center. Jeff didn't know how many of the crew were summoned. He wryly considered asking if he should bring Cosmos. Marie announced that her presence was also requested. He was flabbergasted when he and Marie walked into the conference room. Sitting at the head of the table was someone Jeff had hoped not to see again. Tami Graves rose, smiling, and glided toward him and Marie. She encircled them in a wide embrace. "The Living World rejoices at your union," she intoned. Gimme a break, Jeff thought, forcing himself to vanquish the sarcastic expression about to claim his face and replace it with a plastered smile. He drew Marie close to him, trying not to smirk.

Marie regained her composure first. "What a lovely thing to say," she murmured graciously.

Tami grinned, slowing releasing them. "It's true. And I'm pleased that you came to recognize and fulfill the extraordinary bond between you."

The other team members crowded into the room. Chris Mills and Mannie Patel nearly stumbled into each other gawking at the beautiful young woman. Lana Adams cast a skeptical eye. These three had never seen the human persona of TuMa'Aye Gra'Vay, Queen of the Realm. Tall and graceful, she had long, auburn hair with fiery red highlights and an oval face dominated by luminous green eyes and supermodel bone structure.

"Let's get settled. We have a lot to discuss," Bailey MacIntyre boomed.

The group arranged themselves around the table. The air crackled with suspense.

MacIntyre stood. "We have a special and honored guest. Most of you have never met the Synon we affectionately call Queen of the Realm." A collective gasp was heard as if it had been scripted. "In her human persona TuMa'Aye Gra'Vay is known as Tami Graves. I'd like you to meet her." He turned an outstretched arm toward Tami. She simply nodded. MacIntyre took his seat and assumed a less formal demeanor. "I'm sure you're curious about Tork's trip to the Everglades. He is still in the Realm working on plans. Tami Graves has graciously given a detailed report on his experience to me and Lew Henderson and will provide a brief outline to you now."

The crew nodded, leaning forward eagerly. Jeff sat with eyes downcast into his coffee cup, still trying to come to grips with the presence of the "woman" who had plundered his mind, led him on, and then revealed that, hey, guess what, I'm not really a woman after all. Sorry. He understood her motivations intellectually but could not reconcile them emotionally.

Tami rose and spoke in a calm voice, "Tork contacted Earth." Another gasp, louder and more astonished, was heard around the table. Tami ignored it. "She is in dire pain and misery. Tork felt her rage and fear. She sees humans as an invasive species destroying her. He tried to engage her, but she rebuffed him. Tork related that he received a strong impression of a phrase, 'only they can help.' Then she was gone with no clarification."

The table sat in shocked silence. Chris Mills wrung the end of his ponytail that flopped over his shoulder, bug-eyed, almost visibly twitching, finding it hard to not yell out "The Earth really is alive–and we're killing it!"

Jeff and Marie exchanged glances, Jeff shaking his head and performing his ritual actions of blowing out a breath and raking a hand through his hair.

Tami kept talking, ignoring the stunned humans. "Who are *they*?" The people looked at each other uncomfortably. Did she want them to venture guesses?

Tami's pause was not long enough for anyone to respond, even if they dared to. "Tork asked how the Realm could help. He mentioned the Renegade Synons who have closed Passageways in order to cut off Earth from the Realm, all to no response. We must recognize that she was possibly referring to the humans who are the root of her distress. Do any of you have a comment?"

Human eyes darted around the table at each other, then at the Synons.

Jeff dove in. "Did she disconnect because she could no longer maintain the link? Why wouldn't she be specific about who needs to help her?"

Tami shook her head. "I don't know. Tork said the link was very faint. She doesn't speak in words the way you do. Concepts simply appeared in his mind. Earth seemed weak and tired, but also enraged and afraid. She paused, making eye contact around the table. "It is apparent that we face a crisis that needs to be addressed here, as well as in the Realm. MacIntyre tells me that Annilu and Judilay feel strongly that they found a spot where we might reach Earth again. All five of the Synons present will make that attempt soon." She gracefully took her seat.

MacIntyre stood and took control. His eyes pierced those of the Tech crew. "You all have high clearance. You've borne witness to things that can never leave this room. If you have trouble coping with it all, let us know so that we can counsel you. Everyone except Jeff and the Synons can leave now."

All human eyes swiveled toward Jeff as chairs scraped, throats were cleared, and the crew shuffled out. Marie turned and gave Jeff one lingering look.

When the door closed behind his fellow humans, Jeff continued to avoid eye contact with Tami Graves, his mind racing with questions.

Lew Henderson guffawed. "Despite the soundproofed door, I can hear them babbling away out there. And part of it is questioning why Jeff stayed and they were told to leave." Jeff gave him a pleading glance. "Jeff, you're going with us." Jeff sat with mouth hanging open, unable to form words. MacIntyre's voice filled the silence. "I suppose you've been wondering about that little test we did with you and your cat." Jeff sat upright but didn't interrupt, despite sardonic remarks flitting about in his head. "You and Cosmos do, indeed, have a rapport beyond what we understand is common in human-animal bonds. You were right. The two of you communicate much in the same way that we Synons communicate with animals and other forms of life on Earth, and with each other. You're telepathic."

Jeff hadn't thought he could be shocked any more that day. He had been wrong. His mind whirled. What did this mean? He stammered, "Am I a freak?"

All the Synons uttered encouragement at once: "No, no, no! You are unique and gifted."

Henderson held up his hand. They grew quiet. "Jeff, there probably are other telepaths alive right now. We don't know how many and are attempting to identify them. We've enlisted Synons living around the globe to step up their research and home in on specific people who show promise."

"Are we mutants?" Jeff couldn't halt a grin spreading across his face and a quip escaping his lips. "We can be superheroes!"

Tami Graves laughed out loud. The others regarded her suspiciously; she explained. "I conducted a lot of research into popular culture while living here recently. Jeff's remark is clever." She forced him into eye contact. "You know, Jeff, the prospect of a gaggle of telepathic humans working with us does conjure up superhero imagery, but you already are a superhero."

Jeff felt himself blushing until the resentment crept through him. At it again, huh Tami? Queen of emotional manipulation. He broke eye contact.

■   ■   ■

Emma sat in the big chair, her feet straight out in front of her on its seat. It seemed like a long time had passed since Luisa had brought her back to this room where she had slept on the couch the night before. Tears trickled down her face and her breathing was ragged. She had never known despair like this.

The door opened and a stocky man entered. He wore jeans and a shirt of mottled browns and dark greens. He had a scraggly beard and stringy hair. The man peered at her. "So you're the magical l'il gal." He approached her. Emma instinctively drew her knees up and hugged them, recoiling. He stood in front of the chair, looming over her. "So how do we contact these aliens you've been talking to?" He glared at her. Emma didn't understand what he was asking. She tried to speak, but her voice wouldn't seem to work. "Come on, kid. We can make this easy or hard. Your choice." He took a step closer, balling his fist.

She managed a squeak, "I don't understand what you want."

"It's all over social media. You got something going with aliens." He paused and grinned. "But reckon you keep calling 'em fairies."

"Oh. The fairies."

"Yeah. How do you contact 'em?"

"I don't. They come to me or I just know when they are around."

"How can you make 'em come to you?"

"I don't know." She sank as far into the chair as possible. The man's face had reddened and his fist kept clenching.

"I just don't believe you, kid." He looked away a minute as if in thought, then back at her. "Are they in cahoots with anybody else you know of?"

"I don't know what that means."

"Are they working with anybody? Who else knows about them?"

"I don't know." Sobs shook her tiny body.

The man sighed loudly and said a word she didn't understand.

Another man entered the room. He was tall and slim with gray hair, wearing nice clothes. His icy blue eyes glanced at Emma, then at the man. "Any luck?"

"No, Mr. Singleton. I'm not sure what she really knows."

Mr. Singleton looked closer at Emma. "She's pretty young, but we'll have to proceed with the drug. Luisa says she's adept at using it."

Both men left the room. Emma heard the door lock behind them.

■　■　■

South Florida was much more than swamp and wetlands. Its beaches faced both the Atlantic Ocean and the Gulf of Mexico. Once the railroad was extended to encompass it, in the late nineteenth century, this area began attracting vacationers and residents. Sophisticated, modern cities and picturesque hamlets sprang up. Among the residents were workers and professionals who kept the communities running and provided amenities for visitors and the wealthy who kept year-round or winter homes there. Some of the homes were sumptuous compounds, hidden behind high walls, protected by strong security. One of these belonged to a man named Roger Singleton. Independently wealthy, with a shadowy public face, he shunned publicity and the social events coveted by those in the local high society and its hangers-on.

His family wealth had allowed him to build a private enterprise heavily invested in the research and development of robotics. Singleton had numerous patents on components that, individually, piqued no unusual interest in the technology world. He licensed a few, but most were not shared outside his company. His ambition was far-reaching.

■　■　■

MacIntyre's phone buzzed. He glanced at it, looked closer, reading a text. "I must interrupt our planning meeting." He addressed four Synons and one human, his voice grave. "I just got a message. Emma Goodsen has been kidnapped."

"Do you think her abduction is connected to all this?" Jeff asked quietly, his scalp crawling. Memories flashed, recalling his own experiences with the sensation of a presence deep within his own mind and the nagging need for contact with the beautiful woman who had walked into his life as he ate lunch on the last normal day of his life, months ago. Clinically, he reached into his psyche. The need was gone, but as he opened his mind he had to acknowledge a network of connections nestled deep inside. Connections to humans, a cat, and other-worldly beings.

Only an instant had passed. Henderson nodded in response to Jeff's question. "I don't know how or why, but I know that it is."

"This adds urgency to our mission," Tami stated. She locked eyes with Jeff. "Jeff, are you willing to trust us to guide you back through a Passageway?"

Conflicting emotions surged through Jeff, but he answered without hesitation, "Yes."

■　■　■

This time was different. Jeff felt nestled within a protective cloud, conveyed through bliss that ended far too soon. He had been deposited deep in the forest next to a magnificent waterfall with which he was unfamiliar. As Jeff acclimated to the situation, he was shocked to find himself standing alone on the high precipice from which water gushed. An instant of panic subsumed him, replaced by a soothing feeling that he was still surrounded by the protective cloud. It was night, but ambient illumination glowed. The Synons were still in their natural amorphous state, buoying Jeff amidst their unified presence. Jeff felt himself immersed in the rushing water, but he wasn't wet. He floated among sparkling diamonds. He was aware of voices that were not sound, then realized his was among them. Soothing murmurs and pleas to Earth met with turbulence, despair, rage. The voices grew more insistent with a sense of urgency. "You are destroying us. The Realm will cease to exist. We will not be here to protect you. Let us help."

"Only they can help."

"Who?"

"You know."

Then Jeff was again in motion, swept from the glittering waterfall. Once more the burst of bliss, followed by disorientation and a jolt into consciousness. He stood among the five Synons next to the trail leading to their vehicle. A somber mood embraced them.

"Are you all right?" Tami touched his arm.

He flinched slightly. "I think so. Just a bit disoriented." He regarded his companions. "We made contact, didn't we?" They all just nodded. He rushed on. "But we got the same response Tork had. Only they can help. And refusal to say who."

"She insists that we know," Tami replied. The others seemed distant, not acknowledging the conversation between Jeff and Tami.

"Then, you guys must actually know," Jeff stated simply, looking around the group. "If she is so sure you know, you must. You just need to brainstorm and figure it out."

Tami emitted a small chuckle. "So human and so Jeff," she mused. "But I think you're right. We all know."

CHAPTER EIGHT

Emma sat crying in the big chair. Maybe she was having a bad dream and would wake up soon. She missed her family and her home. Emma wondered what had happened to her friend, Sandy. Was she in another big room, in another big chair? Were they asking her strange questions?

Why were these scary people asking her about the fairies? No one else had believed her when she spoke of them. These people seemed to believe her, but they were mean. Did they want to hurt the fairies? A new, hopeful thought struck her. Maybe the fairies could come and help her! She squeezed her eyes closed and concentrated hard, trying to talk to them. She remembered the man in the highway rest area that her daddy had dragged her away from before she could talk to him. She knew he was a fairy. He could help. She tried to remember what he looked like and talk to him in her mind. Her concentration was broken by the door opening.

Luisa entered carrying a tray, which she set down on the table next to Emma. The tray didn't have food or drink on it. It held cloths and a needle like the nurse had used to give Emma vaccinations. It had hurt. Emma recoiled, shrinking into the chair. Luisa pulled a hassock over in front of Emma's chair and sat on it. She took plastic gloves from the tray and donned them. Emma began loudly sobbing.

"I need someone to restrain her," Luisa shouted.

The stocky man in the mottled shirt entered and approached. Luisa moved to make room for him. He grabbed the squirming, squealing girl and jerked her out of the chair onto her feet. "Need an arm?" he asked Luisa.

"Yes. The left one is closest to me. Hold her still."

The man gripped Emma tightly, his body clamped behind her. He held her left arm so that she was unable to move it at all. She could smell him. He smelled bad, like sweat and cigarettes. Luisa stuck her with the needle. It stung. Emma whimpered. Luisa bathed the spot with wet cotton that smelled of alcohol and placed a band-aid over it. She picked up the tray and left the room.

"Okay, kid. You might want to lay down on that couch. If you're lucky you'll get real sleepy." He steered her to the couch. She climbed onto it and curled up in the corner. She hoped he was right. She just wanted to go to sleep. Then maybe she'd wake up and the bad dream would be over.

■　■　■

As soon as he could, MacIntyre called Vera Schechner. He asked her exactly what she knew of the kidnapping, but she had no information. The police were not releasing details other than the child's name and photo and the name of a woman who might have taken her.

"While I've got your ear," Vera said, "do you know anything, on or off the record, about all the hoopla in the Everglades about a flying saucer that was spotted about the time of the storm? Numerous people have reported flashing, colored lights."

Mac chuckled to himself. It might well have been Tork. He was extremely powerful. In that environment his aura could attract attention. "Vera, you know I couldn't tell you anything if I did know something."

"A reporter I fired recently contacted me about it. She thinks there's more to the story. She asked me to consider rehiring her as a freelancer to look into it. Plus, she's whiffed out news that a reclusive rich guy in Naples is hiring a lot of new security for his beachside enclave. That sort of thing always tweaks her interest. And I must admit, mine too."

And mine, MacIntyre thought. Increased security meant something to hide. "Vera, can you do me a big favor? I've got a young man I need to test in the field. I'd like to send him down there to nose around. Maybe he could link up with your reporter."

"An undercover NSA agent?" MacIntyre could visualize her eyebrows knitting with curiosity.

"I wear a couple of hats," he drawled. "Can you get me more on this guy whose beefing up security? Something about that tickles the back of my mind."

"Well, a child was recently kidnapped in central Florida," Vera stated. "I think I'll give Suki another chance. Maybe I fired her too hastily. She has the nose of a bloodhound. I'll get you her contact info. Please keep me in the loop. I don't want her and your newbie tripping over each other."

"Will do. Thanks, Vera. And please don't air anything about the security issue until our people have been able to look into it."

"Of course I wouldn't." She sounded indignant.

After they'd disconnected MacIntyre sat musing. The hardest part was coming.

* * *

MacIntyre and Henderson found Jeff sitting on a bench gazing at the water flowing rapidly from the small dam upstream of the Tech Center. "Excuse me for interrupting your meditation," Henderson said quietly as he sat down next to his friend, while MacIntyre sat on Jeff's other side.

Jeff smiled wistfully. "Too little time to commune with nature." His expression turned. "So why have the two of you hemmed me in?"

MacIntyre spoke. "How'd you like a little trip to the Everglades for us?"

"What! Wasn't Tork just there?"

"Yes. He went to the Realm afterward, as you know. There are a couple of things we need you to check out."

"Me? You aren't going too?"

"We need to stay here and help Tami recall the Synons who responded to help us against Bandela. We want a large gathering to convene and attempt to reach Earth in unison."

Jeff was incredulous. "I've never been in that area. What am I supposed to do?"

MacIntyre answered. "You went through the police academy and know investigative techniques. Plus, we have some technical equipment that might help you."

"But I repeat. What am I supposed to do?"

"There are reports of a UFO sighting at the time of the hurricane, with flashing colored lights. People are convinced of it, even that it was connected to the storm. We think it might have been Tork transforming to or from his natural state. He's extremely powerful, and in that environment his aura could create quite a spectacle, but it might not have been Tork. We just need you to nose around, talk to the locals, maybe pretend you're a UFO enthusiast. See what you can learn."

"Wouldn't a Synon be better at that?" Jeff was suspicious about their motives.

"There are no Synons available who could pull it off. As we said, you've had some police training."

"Cursory. I'm a tech geek, remember?" Jeff growled. He tried to rise.

Henderson grabbed his arm. "Jeff, we need you. There could be more going on down there than the UFO stuff. The kidnapped girl could be in the vicinity."

"Then call the police down there!" He again tried to stand up. Henderson gripped his arm.

MacIntyre interjected. "A reporter working for YCN has discovered someone down there who's hiring a lot of security staff. That might mean he's trying to hide something. Could be anything, but since little Emma Goodsen was recently kidnapped in central Florida, there is the possibility that he could be holding her. That's too vague for law enforcement. We'd like you to meet the reporter and check it out, then get back to us on it."

"Who do I say I am?" Jeff raked his hand through his hair.

"I'll establish an ID for you, solid enough to withstand scrutiny. We'll work it out together."

Jeff sat back, hands between his knees. "You aren't going to let me off the hook, are you?"

"We're wasting valuable time." MacIntyre rose, pulled Jeff up and began steering him toward the building. "Let's get started."

■   ■   ■

Marie was upset that Jeff was going somewhere on a secret mission that he couldn't tell her about. "Aren't I a member of this team? Don't I have clearance?" she demanded.

"You have NSA clearance. I think this is a Synon mission. I'm probably just drafted because I know about them." He turned to enter their bedroom. "I've gotta finish packing. I'm on a tight schedule." She didn't follow him.

Jeff felt terrible keeping secrets from Marie. She did have high clearance, but where Synon business was concerned she didn't rank.

In addition, he was unsure of why his presence was needed on this mission. Jeff was uneasy with all the talk about his being "special" and felt like they were grooming him as their tool. Bitterly, he recalled Tami Graves. These Synons had no compunction about using people for their own purposes. The attitude they exuded was that theirs was a higher purpose, the highest of purposes, and whatever they had to do to achieve their goals was acceptable. Hypocrites.

Jeff was still trying to process the experiences of going through Passageways and what that might mean. According to these Synons, in all human history there was no record of a person doing that. How could he be so different from all those billions of humans?

Granted, he had linked somehow with Tami when she was in the computer system battling the Renegades. And they had both watched their hands reach for each other in her first Renegade cyber encounter while he was online investigating them. He was probably not the first or only telepathic human. It might be more common than science had ascertained. Incidents were probably just not recognized, or accounts believed. Maybe the reason he was the first to go through a Passageway was that they just hadn't ever tried it before. His mind churned, seeking rationales. Then he remembered what had been said about the child, Emma. She was apparently unique and could telepath with Synons. So now they wanted to rescue her so they could use her too. He almost wanted to back out but knew that the girl was in danger. He had to help her if he could.

What he hated most was not being able to tell Marie about going through Passageways. They had vowed not to keep secrets, but this was one he had been forced to swear he would not reveal. Now he was about to embark on a new secretive experience.

Jeff sighed his signature exhalation, blowing out through his mouth. He finished packing his small bag and looked around the cozy room. He hoped he'd be back to it soon.

■　■　■

Emma lay sprawled on the couch, asleep. Roger Singleton stared down at her. "Why didn't you wake her up before I got here? My time is valuable," he snarled at Luisa.

The woman frowned and began shaking Emma. "If she's completely awake the drug won't work. It's not really a truth serum, you know. It will just make it easier for her to talk and tell the truth without thinking about what she's saying."

Emma's eyes rolled open. She whimpered. "Sit her up," Singleton ordered. Luisa complied. Emma was limp. Her eyes closed again.

Luisa slapped her face. "Don't sleep!"

Singleton loomed over her. "Emma! What's your last name?"

Emma looked up at him in confusion. "Goodsen."

"How old are you?"

"Five."

"Do you have fairy friends?"

"Oh yes." A small smile curled her droopy lips.

"Can you ask them to come visit us here?"

"I don't know how to do that." She tried to lie back down. Luisa quickly grabbed her, sat her up, and placed sofa pillows around her.

"Have they visited you other places?"

"Yeah!" She smiled again, perking up a bit.

"Can't you call them somehow?" Singleton was becoming more and more irritated. "How about just thinking about them real hard and asking them to come into your thoughts. Can you try that?"

"I can think about them and ask them in my head to come here, but they might not come."

"Try it now," Luisa said softly. "Picture each one you want to come. Then think real hard, imagining them right here with you."

"Okay." She closed her eyes tightly and her face squeezed up, her lips pursing. "Lady Fairy. Mr. Fairy. Please come help me!" Emma muttered.

Singleton began pacing. "Keep doing that," he commanded.

Time passed. Emma tired. "I need to go to sleep," she mumbled.

"Let's try another tack." Singleton hissed. "When they visit you do they come in a vehicle of some kind? Like a spaceship?"

"No. The lady just appeared next to me in my car. I had heard her talking before I saw her. She didn't stay but a minute."

"What other fairies have you seen?"

"Well, I don't know for sure he was a fairy, but I could hear in his head."

Singleton stopped pacing. "You could hear in his head?"

"Yes. I didn't hear him talking but his head and my head were together."

"What exactly did you perceive?"

"What?"

■　■　■

Jeff was taken to a hidden mountain airstrip and hustled into a small plane with a taciturn pilot. When they landed at an airstrip that seemed to be as equally hidden in the flatlands of southern Florida, he was summarily ousted from the plane and greeted by a man who didn't introduce himself. He simply said, "This truck," pointing to a dirty pickup, "is yours. I'll drive you to the campground where you'll be staying." He flung Jeff's bag into the back of the truck and headed for the driver's seat, obviously expecting Jeff to get into the passenger side.

"Campground?" Jeff knew he needed a low profile, but he had expected at least a motel.

"It's at Collier-Seminole State Park on the Tamiami Trail. That's near the area where you'll poke around." Jeff nodded, expecting more explanation, which he got. "You went over maps and a plan before leaving. There are more maps and info in the camper. Take a look at this GPS." He pointed to a portable unit on the dash just to the left of the steering wheel. "It looks like a regular plug-in." He pointed to the cord winding down to the cigarette lighter where it was inserted. Jeff nodded again. "It's a lot more than it looks like. We'll be able to track you everywhere this truck goes."

"Why?" Jeff didn't like the idea of someone knowing his every move.

"Your security." Jeff nodded, wondering what they might know that he didn't. And wondering who "they" were. Obviously, there was a team here that would be monitoring him. At least that should make him feel a little better. Help would be nearby. But he still didn't like the notion of his every action being tracked.

The man continued. "It's also a two-way radio. You can press this button," he pointed at an unmarked button on the outer frame, "to talk to us. If we want to talk to you, you'll hear us. Look in the glove box." Jeff complied. It held a plastic envelope with registration and insurance papers and a cell phone, which Jeff assumed he should remove. "Looks like a regular mobile phone," the guy intoned, "but it's got enhanced GPS. Keep it on you all the time and leave it on. It's another two-way communication device, plus a lot more. There's a booklet about it on the camper laptop. We have some more technical goodies there also."

"Cool," Jeff said. "Guess you know I'm a techie."

"That's good. You'll get the hang of the equipment fast and appreciate how it can be of use."

They drove what seemed like quite a way. Jeff took note of the passing scenery, which included a few small eateries, gas stations, tourist shops, and fish camps. He supposed he would soon be stopping to talk to whoever would listen in him. The road was straight, flat, and bordered with swamp and trees, including palms, and scrub.

Jeff was pleasantly surprised by the park and its campground. It was beautiful, good-sized, with water and lush greenery. It was partly within what was called the great mangrove swamp of southern Florida. He had never seen those unique trees in person. They had large rounded green tops and trunks sitting on tangles of above-ground grayish roots that looked like tendrils. The tendrils formed a base for each tree, giving some the look of trees walking on sticks. A river also traversed the park. Jeff hoped he'd have some time to explore this fantastic place a bit. Wistfully, he thought of Marie and how much she'd enjoy it.

The man was speaking again, jolting Jeff back to reality. "It's an ordinary camper, with water, sewer, and electric hookups. He was opening the door and leading Jeff into the small travel trailer set up next to a picnic table surrounded by a few trees. A waft of cool air met them. "We turned on the AC to let it cool off in here." Jeff followed him up the two steps and into the compact, attractive space. "Everything you'll need." The man swung his arm around. Jeff noted the tiny but well-equipped kitchenette and a booth-style table with facing benches. "Couch opens to a full bed." The man nodded at the built-in couch stretching from wall to wall. "There's a small bathroom here, but there's also a nice clean bathhouse nearby with larger fixtures and showers." The miniscule room behind the door looked like a slightly enlarged airplane facility, but in addition to a small toilet and sink there was a shower, barely large enough for an adult to stand in. But nice to have.

The man led him to a corner, almost hidden behind the tall back of one of the benches facing the table. A small desk with a chair held a laptop computer, wi-fi router and several other pieces of electronic equipment. "We've installed upgraded secure internet and Wi-Fi. You'll find a folder on the computer desktop with instructions." He opened a small drawer in the desk and took out some things. "Let's go sit at the eating table so I can show you these." They sat facing each other.

Jeff found himself blurting, "Do you have a name I can call you?"

The man actually smiled. "Just call me Bill."

Bill showed Jeff several electronic items, including eye-glasses containing a video camera in the frames and a micro-phone embedded in a gold earring stud. He suggested that Jeff begin wearing the stud and glasses immediately so locals would be accustomed to seeing him that way. The eyeglasses darkened in sunlight. Bill demonstrated how to activate the gadgets and upload contents onto the computer. "If you record anything we or MacIntyre should know of right away, follow the instructions to send it."

"I know what Mac would want to see, but how do I know what to send you?"

Bill looked at him. "If it's something that needs urgent attention or puts you in danger."

Jeff swallowed. "I get the picture." He again wondered what he was walking into.

"Guess that about does it. Any quick questions?"

"Do you need a ride?"

A small grin cracked Bill's face. "Yeah. You're going to drive me to Naples."

■　■　■

Naples was a lovely Gulf Coast city with an upscale Florida look—cosmopolitan, unlike the area he'd seen near the Everglades. Bill showed him the easiest way to get in and out of the city and had Jeff drop him at a restaurant in a highway strip mall. He didn't invite Jeff to join him, even though it was dinnertime. Instead, he told Jeff about a little place he might want to grab a bite on the Trail and start asking questions. Jeff balked inwardly. Tired, he wanted to sink into the lawn recliner outside his trailer with a beer, and maybe take a nap. But he remembered that a child was missing and he might be able to get a lead on her location.

■　■　■

"Hey. Give me a shrimp po' boy and fries. And a beer. Thanks." Jeff nodded at the middle-aged woman behind the counter.

"Sure, honey. Just a jif." She grinned, revealing a gap where a front tooth should have been.

Jeff removed his ball cap and laid it on the counter. He wondered idly if he should have activated the mike in his ear stud. "Glad to see you open after that storm. Don't look like you got any damage," he drawled. He hoped his Appalachian accent was compatible here.

"We'as real lucky." She placed a bottle in front of him. "Looked like most o' the damage was way out in the 'glades. A few fishin' shanties got tore up and water was over the road in some places, but that ain't nothing new."

"Yeah, heard they was some strange stuff that night." He sipped the beer.

Her back was to him as she prepared his meal, so he turned on the microphone. She might be a trove of information. "Weird. Real weird. Some guys that was fishin' out there seen it. Looked like...well, I ain't gone spread crazy stories."

"I heard tell they seen a spaceship." There. That gave her a hook to bite.

"That tale's sure spreadin'."

"You know either of the guys who seen it?"

"Pauley Moffit an' Parrish Ford." She stated it as if he obviously knew them.

"Okay."

Jeff was glad the mike was recording but decided not to press for any more information right then, eating in silence. He hoped to blend into the laid-back ambience of the Everglades area in the guise of an itinerant handyman, utilizing skills and experience he had gained working while he was in college.

■　　■　　■

The place where the "alien" light show had been seen was along the southern end of U.S. 41, the Tamiami Trail, sometimes called Alligator Alley, snaking through the Everglades. The next day Jeff drove east from the campground, stopping at every small hole-in-the-wall establishment he came across. They were few and far between but offered opportunities to mingle with the locals and soak up current lore, like the combination gas station-café where he was told who had seen the "aliens" the night before. A lot of people were still talking about the "aliens." The story was taking on more and more elements, as happens with rumors and circulating tales of strange events. Several strands related accounts of fishermen witnessing a spaceship ringed with bright colored lights sinking below the tall cypress trees. They heard no sounds, so reckoned that the ship didn't crash but simply landed. They attributed the sudden hurricane conditions to atmospheric disturbance caused by the craft, disregarding scientific data that had tracked the storm's sudden turn toward them. Jeff feigned agreement with the sentiment that the government and media were hiding knowledge from the public. Jeff found it hard to keep a straight face at times. The tales were outlandish, but not as out-landish as the probable truth, not aliens from another planet, but a being comprised of energy from another universe. He was still amused by the image of Tork whooping it up in the Everglades.

Jeff also asked if anyone was looking for help but got no nibbles. When he got back to his camper he called the reporter Mac said had dug up something interesting, Suki Kurosawa. She suggested they meet the next day in Naples.

■ ■ ■

They met at the pier that jutted into the serene Gulf of Mexico. He told her to look for a tall, dark-haired guy in big-rimmed glasses and a gold earring stud. She said she was easy to find: a petite Asian with long black hair, in a big floppy beach hat. He found her leaning on the railing at the entrance to the pier. They introduced themselves and she suggested they stroll.

"I've been cultivating some high rollers here. Can't be seen hobnobbing with the likes of you." She took in his scruffy T-shirt and jeans. "Plus, we can talk more openly. Never know who might be within earshot."

"Yeah. I probably had the best end of it, cultivating the low rollers, mostly decent people just trying to make a living. So what are you on to?"

"First you. I'm curious about what you might have dug up about the alleged flying saucer."

Jeff remembered Mac's briefing. Suki didn't know about Synons. He had to be careful not to let anything slip. "Everybody's still buzzing about it. But it does sound fishy."

"Found anything?"

"Got names of two guys who supposedly saw the light show. I'll track them down."

"Pauley Moffit and Parrish Ford?" He nodded in surprise. She continued, "Good luck finding them. They've vanished."

Jeff stared at her. "Vanished? Like abducted?" His eyebrows rose.

She snorted. "More like hiding out. Or hired by Roger Singleton to work security at his compound."

"What do you know about that guy? Mac...the people I work for want to know everything they can."

She peered at him. "So who is it you are working for?"

"Legit. Can't say more. A friend of your former boss. She gave him your contact info."

"Yeah. She told me about you too. Also said you're working with a good friend of hers that I need to trust. So. Singleton's a shadowy industrialist. He apparently invested old family money into robotics and got even richer. His company is private and doesn't bother with PR."

"You've learned that he's building up his security team?" She nodded. "Any idea why?"

"Not yet. I'm trying to get an invite to a big charity party he's holding soon. He keeps a pretty low profile but occasionally does a big charity event."

"It's not open to anyone who buys a ticket?"

"No. Invite only. The top echelon of society and local government. Strange combo."

"Maybe the additional security is for that event."

"That's the story he's putting out."

Jeff was silent a moment. "Maybe I could get a job there."

"Worth a try."

"How are interested people able to get in touch with him?"

"It's strictly been word-of-mouth. I can ask around."

"Okay. Meantime I'm going to ask about Moffit and Ford, maybe hit two birds with one stone. What do you know about them?"

"They run an air boat business. Don't know what they call it."

"I'll do some research. My cell is on all the time. Text or call if you get something."

"Will do. Same with me. Jeff, just be careful. We don't know what we're stepping into."

CHAPTER NINE

"There you are!" Marie found Judilay slouched, human style, in front of a smart television screen in the Tech Center's lounge. "You're watching old *Star Treks?*"

"Yes. Jeff referred to this television program on several occasions. He says almost all of its science fiction innovations are now realities. He showed me how to find it on a streaming service. The most interesting thing to me is its portrayal of human values and how these characters struggle to maintain them in the face of dangerous and contradictory situations."

Marie grinned broadly. "Could you pause and come back to it later? I have an interesting proposal for you."

"Just give me fifteen more minutes to the end of this episode. I don't want to lose the continuity."

"Okay. I'll be out on the deck. Annilu will be joining us there."

Annilu and Judilay both appeared at nearly the same instant. Of course, they synchronized timing to arrive at the appointed moment. Annilu had fabricated a new outfit that better suited the late summer weather. She wore what looked like cotton cropped pants and a short-sleeved blouse, both of a pale green color. Her feet were clad in sensible brown leather-look sandals. She wore the same brown ponytail that did nothing to enhance her persona's plain face that bore no trace of makeup.

Judilay persisted with his African-Caribbean style in a colorful dashiki and jeans. His shoulder length hair with its elaborate dreadlocks swayed as he walked. Both stood as if at attention in front of the lounge chair on which Marie reclined in the shade of the building overhang. Why me? She grumbled to herself. Why was I yet again asked to show these two how to seem like real people? Just as she was about to tell the two young Synons to take a seat Lana Adams sauntered out of the door wearing baggy shorts, tank top, and floppy straw hat. Spotting them she turned to join their group. "Ain't leisure time grand? What're y'all up to?" She took one of the chairs at the round table near Marie's lounger. The table's center sported a large umbrella that Lana shifted slightly to throw her face into shade. She quipped, "Black skin burns the same as white. Remember that newbies." Her eyes swept over Judilay, who opened his mouth to speak but Marie beat him to it.

The proverbial lightbulb had flashed on in Marie's mind. "Kids," she motioned to the two Synons, "have a seat. I'm so glad to see you, Lana. I think you might be interested in what we're about to discuss." All three leaned forward eagerly.

"While Jeff's away we have a little down time to take advantage of. It's been suggested that I might—and now I'd like to include Lana in this venture—show you two around a bit more and give you some pointers on fitting in better."

"We don't fit in right?" Judilay looked crestfallen.

"You haven't had an opportunity to mingle with a variety of people in a city. We're going on an outing to Asheville. We can even stay overnight in a quaint bed and breakfast. It will be a lot of fun."

"I'm in!" Lana exclaimed. "Judilay, do you mind tagging along with three women?"

"I'd be delighted." He beamed at her.

"Okay. Let's get going," Marie said. "I just have to pick up my things. Chris will stay in our cabin with Cosmos." She smiled expansively at Lana. "I'm so glad you're coming." Another den mother to help me wrangle those two, she thought wryly.

      ▪   ▪   ▪

A scenic drive along narrow, winding roads led to an interstate that dumped them suddenly into a busy downtown, leaving the two newbies a bit discombobulated. Marie drove through streets lined with buildings exhibiting a variety of architectural styles. Storefronts displayed shops, boutiques, restaurants, bars, and galleries with colorful, artistic windows. Sidewalks and outdoor cafes bustled with people. At a wide intersection Marie pointed out the art museum and a square that hosted myriad events. She drove along more picturesque streets to circle Grove Arcade, a historic multistory building that had been revamped to house offices and businesses with street front entrances and more businesses and sidewalk cafes. She pointed out the several notable buildings boasting the Art Deco style popularized in the 1920s and 1930s, encompassing modernism with sleek lines, glass and metals like chrome and aluminum, along with characteristic angular ornamentation, particularly at the tops.

"The city's so dense!" Annilu exclaimed. "So manmade."

Lana drawled. "You should see New York."

"Could we?" Judilay asked enthusiastically.

"Maybe it'll be in your future," Marie replied. "Let's get you used to this level of urbanity first. This city is comparatively small with a compact downtown."

"Nestled among mountains. So charming," Judilay mused. "Does my persona fit here?"

Just as Marie was about to assure him it did, Annilu snapped, "You draw too much attention to yourself. How will you answer questions about your origins if asked?"

"I hadn't thought that far ahead," he admitted. "I did some research. I like the cultural connotations my persona presents. Did you know that dreadlocks have been worn by varied cultures throughout history? Even Vikings! The dashiki is African and was adopted by African-Americans and hippies."

"That's not a personal background." Annilu scowled at him.

"I just liked the look and the cultural references. I haven't thought about my persona's own history," Judilay muttered. He peered at her. "Do you have a personal identity history?"

"Not as yet. Until we both do, we should avoid conversations with people," Annilu proclaimed.

They had parked in a garage and were strolling along the narrow alley-like thoroughfare called Wall Street.

Marie and Annilu stopped to peruse a menu in the window of a vegetarian restaurant while Judilay and Lana lagged behind chattering. Deep in conversation they stood in the middle of the sidewalk. Suddenly a young man with a shaved head bumped roughly into Judilay. "Hey, spade, you don't own this sidewalk!"

Judilay was nearly knocked off his feet. "Oh, I'm so sorry," he murmured.

The young man scornfully ran his eyes over Judilay and Lana. He barked a laugh. "You two are a hoot. He's got the long hair, she ain't hardly got none. Looks like y'all switched sexes, 'cept the spade should be wearing the long skirt."

Judilay was visibly perplexed; Lana was furious. "What century are you from, kid?" she snarled.

"Y'all ain't worth the breath." He spat on the sidewalk. "Shoulda known I'd run into types like you here. But my buds was just itchin' to drink at all these breweries." He shook his head, spat again, and strode on, shoving some other strolling sightseers out of his way.

Lana pulled Judilay up against a building. "I'm so sorry you had to experience that so soon," she said. "He's not typical of Asheville. It's a diverse, peaceful city. He was a visitor."

"Why was he so rude?" Judilay asked. "And why did he call me a spade?"

She sighed. "Long story. Let's have a private talk tonight after dinner."

His face perked up. "I'd really enjoy that," he said smiling.

■   ■   ■

Marie and Lana took their two charges to a popular downtown tapas restaurant for dinner and ordered multiple small plates of delectable fare. "Can y'all drink alcohol?" Lana asked the two Synons. "They have good cocktails here."

Annilu pursed her lips. "Tami warned us that we can't process it into energy as easily as we do food and non-sugary beverages," she replied.

Judilay interjected. "The guys have shared beers with me. It made it harder to maintain my focus. I felt kind of like my persona was going to dissipate."

"Better skip it for them," Marie declared. She looked at the two. "It's perfectly acceptable to simply say you don't drink if someone offers you alcoholic beverages. That seems safest."

"Maybe we can experiment with the team," Judilay said wistfully.

"Perhaps." Lana rolled her eyes. "Please excuse me, but I must have one of their Margaritas. How about you. Marie?"

"I'm driving. I'll pass."

The dinner was convivial and relaxed. The two human women realized that they weren't really providing social practice with strangers, but the Synons were comfortable with the two of them. It was apparent that they needed some private tutoring and role playing before they could be trusted to engage in conversation with strangers.

When they arrived at the bed and breakfast all were tired, but Judilay hadn't forgotten the unpleasant encounter he and Lana had earlier in the day. "Could we have that talk now?" he asked her. Marie's eyebrows rose and Annilu looked cross.

Lana explained briefly what had happened and that she needed to explain it to Judilay.

"Why not with me also?" Annilu demanded.

"It concerns his choice of persona," Lana replied. "You wouldn't have the same experience we had."

"I knew that persona would cause him trouble! It's just too flamboyant."

"That's not the issue." Marie took her arm to steer her towards the stairs. "I'm exhausted. Let's go on up to our rooms.

We can tell you about it tomorrow." Annilu reluctantly accompanied her. Marie was perplexed by Annilu's behavior. Peeking back over her shoulder at the other two as they strolled into the small, private library off the main room, she looked jealous. There was so much to learn about these complicated creatures.

The next morning at breakfast Annilu pounced. "So, Judilay, do you now better comprehend that young man's behavior yesterday?"

He replied, "It seems Synons have overlooked the pervasive human trait of prejudice toward those who are different from them in some way. We've always been aware of its cruel consequence in their treatment of other animals but neglected to see it as a root cause of so many human conflicts. They seem to have a deep-seated need to designate others as inferior so that they can then demonstrate their perceived superiority through persecution and harm, even destruction. It's quite appalling."

"I still don't understand," Annilu persisted.

Lana looked at her with something like disbelief. "Skin. It's my skin color and the skin color he chose."

"Skin color?" Annilu peered at Lana. "Oh, your skin is of a darker hue. I didn't even notice." She turned to Judilay. "How did you realize that you should fabricate darker skin for the persona you chose?"

"As I said, I was just fascinated by this hairstyle that has been worn by many cultures over time but most recently has been associated with people of this skin tone. I like the colorful comfort of the dashiki. I suppose I was behaving like people do by just reacting to appearances. I plan to do some deep research into history now."

Marie was silent. She wanted to discuss this with Henderson, who himself had selected a persona exemplifying a culture that had been treated as sub-human and nearly exterminated by the Europeans who usurped their land. Synons couldn't possibly be so unaware of this dark side of humanity. Perhaps Judilay hadn't been properly prepared in the Realm for this mission.

Judilay continued babbling. "I want to learn more about all the varied human cultures. I do know that this look brings me joy." He noticed Lana watching him. "Your smile is so beautiful!" he gushed to her. He turned to the others. "Lana told me something about growing up near the lovely city of Charleston. I hope she'll take me there for a visit." His gaze brought a slight blush to Lana's dark complexion.

Marie watched. It brought up unpleasant memories of the strange and awkward relationship that had developed between Jeff and Tami Graves.

■ ■ ■

The day had been unproductive. The few places Jeff found open were nearly empty. No one was talkative. It was late afternoon, around quitting time for workers, as he sauntered into what some would have called a beer joint. A number of varied vehicles in its gravel parking lot suggested customers. Jeff pulled his ball cap low on his brow and slouched, hands deep in his pockets as he walked in. His eyes darted up from under the cap's bill, assessing the men who sat at the bar and in a few booths with threadbare upholstery. Ages ranged from young to old; all were white, in jeans or work clothes, most smoked cigarettes or cigars. He suppressed a cough. How did they breathe in that haze? Mingled with the acrid reek of smoke Jeff smelled beer, mildew, and faint whiffs or urine. Lighting was poor. Country music emanated from an antique jukebox. The place was small, cramped. He glanced toward the back, searching for a door amid the shadows. No bright red "exit" signs. His skin prickled. Be cautious. He moved up to the end of the bar.

The bartender glanced at Jeff and nodded but took several minutes to get around to moving over to him. He looked like a stereotypical Hollywood barkeep: burly, multiple tattoos decorating bulging biceps. "What can I get you?" He eyed Jeff appraisingly.

"Whatever beer you got on tap."

The man didn't acknowledge but merely turned and walked away. A few of the men closest to Jeff looked at him. He caught the eye of one and nodded amiably, careful not to smile. They merely turned back to their glasses.

When the barkeep brought his beer, Jeff spoke up quickly, but quietly. "I'm lookin' for a guy I was told might have a job for me."

The barkeep arched an eyebrow, shrugging. "So?"

"Pauley Moffit."

Steely eyes bore into him. "Where'd you get that name?"

"Guy I met a couple months ago said he might be expanding his airboat business. Thought he might need some help."

The man who sat closest to Jeff, a couple of stools away, jerked his head around. Jeff forced himself to look the barkeep in the eye, with his peripheral vision aware of the other man.

"What you been doing since?" The barkeep gave the other guy a sideways look.

"Well, I lucked into a gig on a deep-sea fishin' boat outta Naples for a while, but their business really dropped off this summer with all the bad weather and they let me go." He took a big gulp of beer, smacked his lips, and grinned. "Good brew." The yarn seemed like a way to get attention, but Jeff had no idea of what he'd do if offered a job. He had no experience with boats. He was hoping it might lead to a job with Singleton's security crew.

From the corner of his eye he saw the two men next to him watching. The barkeep turned toward them. "You might ask these two here." Then he was off helping another customer.

Jeff got up and strolled to an empty stool next to them. "Mind?" he asked gesturing his beer at the stool. The one next to him grunted. Jeff took it as assent. He slowly placed his beer on the bar and sidled onto the stool. "Jeff McCarthy." He held out his hand. The other man didn't take it, so he let it drop to his side.

"So you're lookin' for Pauley Moffit. He nor his partner Parrish Ford been around since that storm. Some people think it kilt 'em, but others say they was around talkin' about it afterwards. Saw some strange stuff. But all the same. Nobody's seen 'em since."

"Did their business get destroyed?"

"Naw. The shack they work out of is still there, and one boat was tied up but partially sunk. Still layin' on its side in the water, far as I know. No idea about the other boats."

The man next to him had been twitching and finally burst out, "Some people think they got abducted by aliens. They was real weird stuff goin' on that night."

The first man scowled at him. "Aaron, you gotta be careful who you talk that stuff to."

Jeff grabbed the opportunity. "Aw, you don't hafta worry about me. I heard all about them lights. Too many strange things been going on. An' people disappearin'. Did'ja see the reports of that little girl from central Florida? The one who'd been on TV sayin' aliens talked to her." He deliberately twisted the truth. "They said someone she knew took her, but then they couldn't find anything on 'em. It's either aliens or the damned government. Maybe both workin' in cahoots." Jeff hoped he wasn't slathering on the vernacular too thickly.

Both men grinned and nodded. "Ain't that right!" exclaimed the twitchy one. He thrust his hand across to Jeff. "I'm Aaron and this here's my older brother Cliff."

Jeff shook his hand with a grin. "Good to know you both."

"Well looks like you're outta luck at finding a job with Pauley and Parrish," Cliff said.

"Yeah. Too bad. But I can always scrounge up something. I get a little money from helpin' out over at the campground where I'm stayin'. I'm just kinda worried about what happened to them. Maybe I'll poke around a little."

His two companions looked at each other for a long moment. "I wouldn't be doin' that." Cliff's tone bore a hint of threat.

Jeff answered with what he hoped was a knowing look. "Gotcha." He drank down his beer and slapped some bills on the counter. "Maybe I'll see you around." Jeff slid off the stool.

Cliff surprised him. "Hey, you got a phone number? If we learn anything we can call you."

"Yeah. Give me your phone and I'll put it in."

Cliff frowned. "Left it in the truck." He yelled at the barkeep, "Hey, Dykes. Gotta paper and pencil?"

■ ■ ■

Vera Schechner now had a name. The man Suki Kurosawa was looking at was Roger Singleton, an enigmatic visionary who had made a fortune in robotics. She supposed Bailey MacIntyre would ferret out more on that angle. He would also be interested in an odd contradiction she'd found in Singleton's sparse public statements. Several questioned human contribution to global warming and climate change. Why would a man who seemed devoted to science and technology do that? Her experience suggested that money had to be involved. She needed to go deeper into his financial history. Maybe he had hidden investments in the fossil fuel industry or other businesses that profited from the continued denial that they contributed to the warming climate. Public opinion was swayed by propagating the idea of totally natural climate change unaffected by human activity that defied scientific data.

There had to be additional financial incentives from influencing the populace in this direction. Those who were profiting the most, beyond fossil fuel, were disaster recovery and rebuilding companies. Other sectors faced dire situations. The private property insurance companies were struggling as astronomical claims threatened to bankrupt them. Premiums were rising exorbitantly, beyond what many could afford, so the number of uninsured people was increasing. Small businesses that had been destroyed were unable to rebound. Many communities were nearly deserted as residents and business owners found it impossible or unfeasible to rebuild. Agriculture suffered enormously as large swaths of farmland became unproductive and livestock was lost, threatening the food supply. Waterways were polluted, affecting not only drinking water, but agriculture and the seafood industry, tourism, and recreation. Looming was the exorbitant cost to government. How long would it be able to cover disaster costs? The situation was worse in poorer countries. Ecological collapse was imminent in many areas. It seemed to Vera that Nature was rapidly losing balance. How had this happened so fast?

Yet rather than taking responsibility and looking for solutions, many people scoffed at science, reverting to modern folklore, attributing natural events to extraterrestrial activity or the supernatural. Mixed in were conspiracy theories like the one gaining momentum relating how world government leaders were working with the aliens in a deal to save themselves.

Vera shook herself out of her rumination, edited and sent her preliminary findings on Singleton to MacIntyre.

CHAPTER TEN

Jeff sent video and audio from his conversation with Aaron and Cliff to Mac, hoping he could dig up more information on them and the two men they had discussed. He did, sending Jeff an email complete with backgrounds and mug shots. All were local. Both Aaron and Cliff were high school dropouts. All had sketchy work histories and run-ins with the police dating back to their teen years, but no convictions. They all scuttled around the edges of various paramilitary groups. Moffit and Ford had been investigated for various cons and jobs for local criminal bosses, including illegal gun and drug trafficking, but without suffi-cient evidence to prosecute. Their business might be a cover for more lucrative illegal pursuits. They were criminal flotsam.

Soon after, a surprise call from Parrish Ford catapulted Jeff into a mysterious and possibly dangerous situation. Ford's employer needed security for a big event at his compound. He wanted to talk to Jeff.

"I'm kinda surprised Aaron and Cliff told you about me," Jeff said to him.

"Well, we did check you out. Looks like you got the kind of talent we might need. Guess you aren't shy about carrying a sidearm, as a security guard, of course. A lot of big shots are attending, and we have to keep 'em safe, you know."

Jeff quickly recalled the background Mac had established for his alias, Jeff McCarthy, remembering it included an arrest, without jail time, for illegally carrying a firearm at a political rally. "Uh," he hesitated, not sure how far to go. "As a bona fide security guard, sure. I'm not risking the slammer, though."

"Sure, sure. Mr. Singleton is a well-respected citizen. That's why we went ahead and called you even with your record. We all do some stupid things when we're young. You also have some other qualifications that will interest him."

"Oh yeah?" Jeff wondered if his comments about aliens around the Trail and Jeff McCarthy's online rants were paying off. "So what's going on that needs beefed up security?"

"Well, Mr. Singleton's pretty rich, and everybody under-stands he needs regular security. But he's throwing a big charity shindig and needs to hire extra. There ain't a lot of qualified talent around here."

"Okay. Sounds like a good gig. Thanks." Ford gave him directions to the compound, including what to say to the guards at the gate. They'd direct him where to go.

Jeff immediately made reports to Mac and the local contacts, asking for direction on how to proceed. Maybe it was a simple security job. If so, it would give him access to the compound, but he knew he'd have to be careful about using any gadgets. Even for employees Singleton would have high tech sensors. Then he called Suki Kurosawa.

■   ■   ■

Singleton had become frustrated with the lack of information coming from the child. He had to hold himself back from hitting her, aware that it would just make her more hysterical. She became distraught, crying so loudly that he was alarmed she would be heard, even though he had made sure Emma was isolated, the only person on the third floor other than those few charged with caring for, watching, or questioning her. There were preparations to oversee for the charity event that he needed to garner favor with people in powerful positions. He had to temporarily stop the interrogation and find another way to get the child to talk. He had assumed that the child would readily prattle on about her alien friends, allowing him to have her dropped off somewhere in another state before the party.

Singleton glowered at Luisa. "Find another drug that works. Now. I don't care what its consequences are as long as the brat tells us what we need to know."

    ▪   ▪   ▪

The mean people left. Emma was alone again, frightened. The drowsiness that had almost claimed her had evaporated, leaving her sobbing, intaking big gulps of air. She felt abandoned. Where was her daddy, the policeman? Why hadn't he come for her and put the bad people in jail? Why had her friend Sandy and her mother brought her here and disappeared? Her mind was a jumble of confusing impressions; although precocious, she was too young for comprehensive and analytic thought so was overwhelmed by emotion.

    ▪   ▪   ▪

Jeff reported to the Singleton compound the morning of the event. It was a beautiful fortress, in the Spanish hacienda style, surrounded by tall stone walls. A wide, elaborate, but heavy wrought iron gate was flanked by two stone guard towers. Jeff stopped, wondering if he was expected to get out of his truck or wait to be approached. The wait was short, but the method of greeting startled him. A voice boomed from a speaker asking for his name and business. He rolled down his window and responded in the general direction of the tower from which the sound came. "Today's password," the voice demanded. Jeff uttered the word he had been given when told when and where to report. The gate slowly swung open. A uniformed man emerged and motioned him forward into the large paved courtyard. To his surprise, he was led to a cavernous garage, built partially underground, quite an engineering feat right next to the beach. Inside another man directed him to park. He got out of his truck and the same man approached and without greeting simply said, "Follow me." Jeff was taken to what looked like a large freight elevator and was told to get off when the door opened. It appeared to only rise one floor. The large door opened onto an open area surrounded by several sets of double doors. One opened and another man appeared; he was tall and muscular and wearing a uniform. He grinned and held out his hand. "Parrish Ford. Good to have you on board. This is a one-time job, but we might want you for additional work. Come on in and meet the other new guys for tonight. There's coffee and pastries. The orientation will begin shortly."

"Good to meet you too. Thanks again for the job." The prospect of more work could be beneficial but was distasteful to Jeff. They shook hands and Ford moved away to speak to someone else. It was a nondescript, windowless room containing several rows of folding chairs facing a large screen. About a dozen men milled about. Jeff sauntered to the refreshment table, poured a cup of coffee, and eyed his companions. All were young, dressed in jeans like him. Then they were told to be seated, and the orientation began. It was a crash course in how Mr. Singleton's security guards should comport themselves among distinguished guests. Courtesy. Good posture. Speak only when spoken to unless instructed otherwise. They were auxiliary, there to help shepherd the guests to where they should be and keep them away from where they shouldn't be, as politely as possible. Jeff was glad to hear that they would not have sidearms but knew that might not hold for additional assignments.

They were told that armed help was immediately available if they pressed a certain button on their communicators. Those devices were explained in detail, with onscreen visuals, after which each man was issued his own, and a practice session was held. They were told that as they left the room they would be given their uniforms. All of their personal belongings would be secured in individual lockers until they were dismissed at the end of the evening when communicators and uniforms would be returned; then they'd be paid and escorted out of the compound. Each would be asked to sign a legally binding nondisclosure agreement. Jeff thought it was a lot of preparation and care for one evening. Some important people must be coming.

The next portion was of most interest to Jeff. A visual tour of the compound, which he was surprised to learn consisted of only one main building, albeit a sprawling one with several wings, each devoted to specific uses, including mechanical, utility, and maintenance. The main level, above the garage, contained the public reception and dining areas, with sliding glass walls facing the expansive veranda, part of which was covered, with the outer area facing the pool and low sea wall opening on to the Gulf. Guests were to be asked not to venture beyond the first floor or the veranda, which was walled on the two sides at right angles to the beach.

Extensive photos were shown of the opulent public area, and each of them was provided a map of it with parameters marked beyond which guests should not stray. The facilitator smiled as he gazed at quizzical faces. "There's a valid reason to keep the guests in the public areas. The decorations there are, for the most part, other than some wall art, superb facsimiles. Worth some money, but not the priceless objects in the family collection housed in the private quarters. Also, Mr. Singleton conducts his business on the second floor, and obviously the curious or those with more nefarious objectives must be discouraged. Mr. Singleton wants to make his guests feel welcome and appreciated, to provide an incomparable evening of entertainment and goodwill. Thus, you each have been selected, in some part, due to your amiable and polite demeanor, coupled with an appearance of implicit ability. You should never be overtly intimidating, but if confronted by an insistent or unruly guest, you can be firm until assistance arrives. Please do make every effort not to touch any guest. Under no circumstances return any friendly or flirtatious overtures. You'll be given a small handbook of instructions to keep in your pocket. Feel free to direct guests anywhere in the public area they ask about."

Jeff was amused by the facilitator's formality. He was beginning to think this whole effort was going to be a waste of time. He didn't relish spending a long evening babysitting snobs.

However, one tidbit of the offered information might be worth it all. Singleton worked on the second floor. It looked like the principal part of the building was three or four floors. It was hard to discern because there were several visible towers, but private quarters might well be on the third floor. That meant that if Emma were held there, she could be almost anywhere. There were probably private, possibly secure, rooms anywhere above the ground level, or even somewhere on the below-ground level beyond the garage. Jeff felt useless.

The day went fast. The orientation took some time, after which each was fitted with a uniform. Then they were taken on a walking tour of the public areas where they would be stationed. Regular guards would man the gate and garage, escorting guests. It was eye-opening. Jeff had never been in such an ostentatious place. There was an immense formal dining room, a library, a screening room, multiple intimate sitting and dining rooms, and the huge open reception area with its soaring ceiling and magnificent glass wall. This was where the buffets and bars would be. A band was setting up in an adjacent ballroom where guests could enjoy dancing. Speakers would carry the music throughout the entire interior and exterior, but at a low volume to encourage conversation. The expansive veranda would contain more buffets and bars. Throughout, comfortable couches, chairs, tables, and seating arrangements would entice beneficial discourse among attendees. This was to be, basically, a huge networking event for the movers and shakers, all of whom were donating a hefty amount for the privilege of attendance. The charitable component was the only positive angle in Jeff's mind. It might be amusing to observe it all. He knew none of them, of course, so would have no insight into who might be schmoozing with whom. He hoped Suki would show up. She would recognize many of them.

The day was long, but the recruits were well treated with breaks, lunch, and dinner before the guests were scheduled to arrive. It would be a late night. They only made small talk among themselves during breaks. None seemed eager to become acquainted on more than a superficial work basis. Jeff learned nothing useful about any of them.

Jeff was surprised that they did not pair the new recruits, but there were enough of them to cover the large area. He was glad to be assigned to the north side of the veranda. He tried to look official and tough, strolling the perimeter from the building to the sea wall overlooking the Gulf of Mexico. It was artfully and subtly illuminated, taking advantage of the night ambience while allowing guests to recognize each other. A caressing breeze carried the scent of the salty Gulf. The array of food and beverages at multiple stations was lavish. Guests tended to gather near them, nibbling and chatting. They were dressed to impress, many women glittering with what he assumed were genuine gems. He fell into a routine, noting activity but not staring. No one approached him. In fact, they acted as if he were invisible. Fine with him.

As the moon rose over the back of the structure, his gaze was drawn upward. The roof was outlined in lunar glow. Jeff surveyed the building. There were two floors above the main one. The visible towers seemed to be behind an expanse of sloping red tile roof. Large windows were swathed in darkness except for one faint light on the third floor. He peered at it intently. The light filtered through closed drapes. Careful not to linger, he resumed his patrol. When he reached his closest point to the window he looked up again, focusing on the light.

"Are you a fairy?" Jeff was jolted by a child's voice. He whirled around, but only adults gathered nearby, drinks in hand. "Did you come to help me?" It was weak but unlike anything he'd ever experienced. It seemed to be inside his head, but unlike a memory or daydream.

"Are you a fairy?" the voice repeated. Jeff's gaze was drawn back to the one lit window above. A palpable sense of connection overwhelmed him. The face of Emma Goodsen, which he had only seen on TV, swam into his perception as if it hung right before him. Looking down, he shook his head. Had they put drugs into his dinner? "Can you help me?" The voice was clear. Jeff felt like he was in a dream but struggled to maintain his professional demeanor. Realizing he'd been standing in one spot, staring upward, he began strolling again, eyes rolling over the crowd. The image of the girl followed.

Jeff's mind was whirling. He recalled the Synons taking him through Passageways, their insistence that he was "special," the tests with Cosmos. Was it true? And was this child like him? Had she been able to find his mind from the many others there? He stopped, peering again at the window and tried to send thoughts the same way he did with Cosmos. "I'm not a fairy, but I'll try to help you. Do you know where you are?"

"In a big house."

"Is the ocean next to it?"

"Yes."

"What else can you tell me?" His military training and experience took control. Logic and focus pushed emotion and speculation aside. "Is there more than one floor?"

"Yes! I rode in an elevator!" Certainty. She was there. Even though she sounded all right he asked the next question with trepidation. "Have they hurt you?"

"They gave me a shot. That hurt."

Drugs. For what purpose? "Did it make you sleep?"

"Yes, but they wouldn't let me. They just kept asking questions."

"About what?"

"The fairies. They think they have spaceships. They want me to call them."

This was shocking. Did Singleton really believe extraterrestrials were visiting and that Emma was in touch with them? Then he had to smirk. Yes. It was true, but not the kind of extraterrestrials that came in spaceships from other planets. What did Singleton want?

Jeff's attention was jerked back by Emma's voice. "Do you have a spaceship?"

He chuckled. "No I don't."

"The mean people think you do." She apparently didn't absorb his statement that he wasn't a fairy.

"The mean people? Can you tell me anything about them?"

"Luisa. She has an accent. Then there are big men."

"What about your little friend and her mother? Did they take you there?"

"I don't know. I fell asleep in their car, and then I was here. But I haven't seen my friend Sandy and only saw Mrs. Johnson once. The other people don't know them."

So her friend's mother apparently did drive Emma there and left. An intermediary, probably using a fabricated identity to get close to Emma. That indicated a preconceived plan. He needed to get in touch with Mac immediately, but how?

Then he spotted Suki Kurosawa winding her way toward him, smiling and nodding at guests she passed. Her eyes met his and her expression changed.

Jeff wanted to reassure the child. "I have to go now, Emma. But I'll still be here in your mind. I'll find you."

∎ ∎ ∎

Suki got invited to the reception at the Singleton Complex as the date of a young social hanger-on who had wangled an invitation. She called Jeff to tell him but wasn't surprised to get his voice-mail. She left a message that she'd be attending the reception. She dressed in glamorous finery that had nearly maxed out her credit card. A slinky black dress matched the sheen of her long dark hair. Makeup deftly applied gave her eyes even more of an Asian slant than her usual no-makeup appearance. This was a time to take advantage of her exotic beauty and well-toned body. Suki's date, Jason, an ambitious realtor, picked her up and chattered all the way to the compound. He told her nothing she didn't already know, despite her attempts to wheedle something useful out of him. She knew she'd have trouble getting rid of him at the end of the evening, but she had a plan to take care of it.

It was dusk as they pulled through the gate of the compound wall, were checked out by guards, and directed to the guest garage at one side. After parking, they were escorted by a guard into an adjacent reception area. As she had expected, a metal detector decorated the door. They were told what metal objects they should remove, not including jewelry. She supposed that the ladies decked out in their finest baubles would balk at being asked to remove them. That meant, however, that the scanners were tuned to bypass certain types of objects. So maybe she could have gotten away with a tiny camera embedded in a necklace or earring, like she had suggested to Jeff. He had firmly warned her not to risk getting caught with surveillance equipment. Suki wondered if Jeff had ignored his own advice.

From there, they were taken through a long glassed-in breezeway to a huge room, which was obviously the primary entertainment area. The far side of it had glass walls that were open to a vast outdoor terrace. Jason continued to chatter as she took in the other guests, trying not to gawk. She interrupted his discourse about previous parties he had attended there. "Can you introduce me to anyone?"

He shut up and looked around. "I recognize several guests but am not acquainted with them. Many others are totally unfamiliar to me. Let's get a drink." Her carefully cultivated escort could turn out to be useless. He steered her toward a bar next to which stretched a long table opulently decorated with more kinds of gourmet food than she'd ever seen.

"Thanks, Jason. I'll have a white wine." Suki took the opportunity to get her bearings and observe the environment. Besides the breezeway entrance, she noted an arched doorway in an interior wall of the room that seemed to lead to a corridor. She touched Jason's arm as he stood at the crowded bar. "Do you know if the powder room is through that archway?"

He looked around the perimeter. "I'm not sure."

"I'll just check it out while you get the drinks. I need to touch up my hair before meeting anyone."

Beyond the archway, Suki discovered not a simple powder room, but a huge, elegant ladies' lounge. Women crowded the outer area that consisted of a long counter from which rose a continuous mirror to the ceiling. Suki managed to find a spot to stand and began smoothing her hair as she gazed at herself. "I guess I'm not the only one with the need to check my appearance before mingling." She laughed, turning to the woman next to her.

The older, elegantly attired woman gave Suki an appraising glance, frowning as she gazed at Suki's dress. "I'm aghast at the rabble they've let in here." She turned and left without another look or word.

So the snobby set is in attendance, Suki thought. Well, the moneyed and influential come in all types. She wondered if she'd have a chance to meet the host and assess his type.

When she exited the lounge, she looked down the corridor on which it was located. It was long, ending at an elevator. Assuming a confident pose, Suki strolled to it, noting that it bore an Art Deco-style curved floor number indicator above the door. Three floors and a basement.

"I'm sorry, ma'am, the elevator is not in use tonight." A male voice spoke courteously, but firmly. She whirled to see a burly, uniformed man approaching. The plush carpet had entirely deadened the sound of his footsteps. She shuddered inwardly as she looked past him to the hallway in which no other people were visible other than a few at the restroom doors at the other end. He could have swiftly strangled her or dragged her into a room! She had to be more alert.

Regaining poise, she tossed her head and smiled up at him. "Oh, I know. I was just admiring this workmanship and design." She looked upward at the Art Deco floor indicator. "My escort will be looking for me, please excuse me." She glided past him, trying to emulate a fashion show runway walk back to the party, wishing she could take off and run.

Suki found Jason conversing with a small knot of men. Touching his arm, she murmured, "Care to introduce me?"

A bit startled, he quickly strove to regain composure and placed his arm around her waist, whispering in her ear. "I really don't know any of them. I just wandered up." He grinned.

One of the men noticed her, running his eyes over her approvingly. "Well, hello there." He almost leered. "Where have you been?"

Suki felt like slime had engulfed her, but she put on an inviting smile. "I just arrived." She extended her hand. "I'm Kim Sawa."

His reply stunned her. "I'm so glad you could come, Miss Sawa. I'm Roger Singleton." He squeezed her hand, locking eyes with her. He was almost a caricature of the distinguished, fit, gray-haired middle-aged man. She chastised herself for not recognizing him from the many photos she'd seen. But she hadn't really looked closely at the small group of men Jason stood among. What a stroke of luck. She noted that her useless escort had not recognized his host either, despite all his boasting of ties to Singleton. He had inadvertently kept the time she'd spent cultivating him from being a total waste.

Her smile was alluring. "It's a pleasure to meet you. Your generous philanthropy is such an important part of this community," she gushed, withdrawing her hand from his grasp. "This is a marvelous place. I'd love to see more of it." Jason made a coughing sound. She ignored him, beaming at her host.

"I'd be glad to give you a tour." He stepped closer and took her by the arm, turning her around and steering her away from the group. She hastily looked back at Jason with a slight shrug and let Singleton guide her.

He led her out of the main reception room, down a short hallway and into a comfortably furnished room filled with art. "Let me show you some of the fine reproductions on display here."

"Oh. These aren't originals?" She looked amazed as she peered at a painting.

"There are some originals, of course. But I couldn't possibly allow my finest art to be displayed in such a public way. I love for my guests to have free range on the first floor to enjoy themselves but, unfortunately, you can't trust everyone. My real treasures are on the floors above, where my private quarters and workspaces are."

She moved closer to him. "Are select guests ever invited up there to see your art?"

"Your perfume is divine," he mumbled in her ear. "It's quite tempting, but no. There are some secluded and private small rooms on this floor, however."

"How convenient. But your art collection is legendary. I was hoping to see at least some of your finer pieces." She forced herself not to move away from him. She could smell the revolting aroma of tobacco on him. Probably from the most expensive cigars.

"Well, uh. There are a few rare finds in my outer office. Let me alert the guards." Singleton spoke into his watch. "Come with me, Kim."

She was led to the elevator and up one flight. It opened onto a large area surrounded by three walls, each with a door in its center. All the doors were closed. Singleton went to the most opulent one made of heavy dark wood in which abstract carvings seemed to swirl. He stood in front of the keypad, hiding it from her. She heard six beeps and the door swung open. As it did, low lights inside came on. Singleton stood aside and motioned her in. Suki swallowed, gripped with anxiety. She wished she had some kind of weapon, then recalled the sharp decorative comb in her hair. And her spike heels. She had had some personal defense training and hoped she could extricate herself from what Singleton clearly had on his mind. It looked like another reception room but this time larger and very well appointed. She supposed this was where he deposited those who wished to confer with him on business matters until he deigned to give them his attention. He led her to a large glass-doored cabinet made of ornately carved wood and pressed a button turning on interior illumination. "Here are a few of my Oriental antiquities." Noting his outdated term for Asian with disgust, she stepped closer, marveling at the sight. Jade sculptures, lacquered Chinese bowls, delicate calligraphy, and what looked like a Japanese Samurai headpiece, among other items.

"I'm speechless," she breathed. "It looks like a museum." He was too close behind her. She felt his breath. She stepped aside, quickly moving around the room as if surveying its treasures. "So what's behind doors number two and three?"

"What?" He looked irritated.

"The other doors opening from the elevator. Is this the center of your enterprise?" She moved toward the door.

Singleton took a few long strides and was again right behind her. "I suppose you could say that. However, due to the proprietary nature of our work, it's off limits."

"I'm just curious, since you're such an obvious genius, about how you work."

He wasn't flattered. "That's also proprietary." He grabbed her arm. "Are you a spy? Who sent you here?"

"Let go of me!" She tried to free herself, but his grip was too strong. "What do you mean spy? And nobody sent me here. I was invited by a friend, and he's probably looking for me right now. I want to go back downstairs." Suki realized she had not planned effectively and put herself in danger with no easy way out. No light had emanated from under the other doors. The floor was quiet. But it would be soundproofed. What if the little girl was quivering behind one of those nearby doors?

"I thought perhaps you'd like to visit my private quarters on the third floor." His voice was softer. He still held her by the arm.

She should say yes. That was likely where the child was. She visualized herself performing martial arts moves she had only practiced with a friendly instructor. Could she protect herself? Anxiety morphed into fear. She thought of the child and forced herself to relax. "Please let me go. I don't like rough stuff, but..." She let her voice trail off. "It never occurred to me that you need to always be wary of spies. Of course, you would. I might be out of my league here." She giggled. "I just thought you were attractive and fascinating."

"You're babbling and wasting my time. What is your fee?"

Suki was flabbergasted. He thought she was a hooker! Maybe that snobby woman in the bathroom had her look pegged right. Had she dressed inappropriately? Yes, she had. Her plan had been to catch Singleton's eye. This was the result. "I...I'm new at this," she stammered. "I'm sure you're generous."

"All right. This way." They went back out to the elevator. She took care to peer around and under the doors and listen for any sounds. Nothing. The elevator opened onto a long corridor on the third floor. He led her toward the opposite end past a number of closed doors. About halfway down she saw it. Dim light seeped from under one door on the right. All others were dark. She looked back to count the number of doors behind it to the elevator. It was the fourth door. Behind it was only silence. This could well be where Emma Goodsen was held. Time to get herself out. How? She was alone with Singleton in a long, empty hallway, two floors up from anyone. She decided to try a ploy.

She stopped. It wasn't hard to make herself begin weeping. "I'm so sorry, Mr. Singleton. I just can't. I know I can't please you. I'm too nervous. You're really out of my league. Can we just go back downstairs? I'm sorry for wasting your time." She sobbed.

Singleton glared at her, his fists balled. Was he going to hit her? She backed away. Should she kick off her heels and dash for the elevator? No. He was tall with a long stride. He'd catch her.

Singleton's face was contorted with anger. He barked a harsh laugh. "Well, this is a first for me." He eyed her. She felt her heart pounding. He growled, "I'm not falling for your scam. If you make up some story you'll regret it. I have the best legal counsel money can buy. Now get out of here."

She turned and ran for the elevator. Relief washed over her as she rushed out on the first floor. She had to try to find Jeff before Singleton's guards located her. Where was he? She raced to the main area, frantically looking around. A few guards stood impassively around the perimeter. No Jeff. She spotted Jason wandering around near the buffet and scurried to avoid him, dashing out onto the veranda. It was more crowded than the indoor area. The music was louder, and the illumination less distinct. Suki pushed into the crowd, trying to avoid all guards except the one she was looking for. She pushed through to the northern end of the veranda, and there in the dimmer light she saw Jeff. He was staring up at the building. A slight glow of light spilled from a third-floor window. As she moved closer Suki was stunned by Jeff's countenance. He looked transfixed.

■　　■　　■

A part of Jeff's mind lingered with the child, but the look of desperation Suki wore drew his attention. She rapidly approached and stopped in front of him, blurting out, "Look stern and move to detain me." She held out her arms as if expecting him to handcuff her.

Bewildered and confused, Jeff muttered, "I'm not allowed to touch guests."

She looked about in panic. "I have to leave right now under guard. You need to be the guard." She stopped his attempt to interject. "Lead me out to the garage. I'll explain later."

Looking like he was still in a trance, Jeff glanced up at the window, reluctant to leave. Suki said sharply, "I think she's there. On the third floor. Now let's go."

He nodded, looked intently back at the window for a moment, then spoke in a loud voice, "Miss, please proceed to the garage. I'll be right behind you."

Before complying she whispered, "Notify Singleton that you're escorting me out."

Jeff looked shocked. "I communicate only with a supervisor," he mumbled, looking at her questioningly, then made the report on his communication device. Both walked in silence through the crowd.

Once they were clear and approaching the garage exit Suki spoke. "I'm fine. I'll order a car but need to disappear quick. I'll be in touch."

"What about the guy you came with?"

"Past tense. My whole gig in Naples."

"But Singleton will be looking for you."

"And won't find me. I don't think Singleton will talk about our little escapade, but I can't take chances."

Jeff's eyebrows rose. "Escapade with Singleton?"

They were walking through the garage. Several guards noticed them and nodded at Jeff. When they reached the gate Suki spoke quietly, "I got to the third floor, saw light from the fourth door from the elevator on the right. Other doors were dark."

"Are you saying you went up there with Singleton?"

"Good. Cabs are lined up in front. I'll be in touch." She dashed to a cab and leapt in.

Jeff stood watching in disbelief, wondering what had happened. But he knew Suki would be all right. Emma wasn't. Did he dare jump in his truck and speed out right then? Or should he stay and contact Mac for instructions? He decided on the latter. He was on site. He knew where Emma was. She had to be rescued.

Fearing that other guards were watching him, Jeff sauntered back through the garage, looking for a dark spot in which to disappear for a moment to contact Mac. When he found a dark corner and was sure no other guards were nearby, Jeff was glad he'd risked wearing his earring stud. Now he removed it and activated the tiny communicator.

No preliminaries. "Jeff?"

"She's here." He concisely related his communication with Emma.

"Are you still on duty?"

"Yeah. Probably a few more hours; then I have to go through some kind of mustering out process."

"Await further instructions. Don't try anything on your own."

■　■　■

Bailey MacIntyre chewed his lip, a habit cultivated over years of emulating human behavior. Now he did it automatically, his mind deeply focused on matters of great significance. Jeff's message that he'd located the kidnapped girl was encouraging but made it priority to devise a way of safely and secretly rescuing her. He had no doubt it could be done. It just required deliberative thought and meticulous planning and execution.

Jeff had calmly related a telepathic exchange between himself and the child, indicating that Jeff was accepting his uniqueness. It added to the mounting evidence of such capabilities worldwide, although still a miniscule portion of the population. This remarkable five-year-old appeared to represent an even more significant phenomenon. She somehow was able to locate a kindred receptive mind in a crowd of people, a mind with which she had never before made contact. If there were others like her it was indeed a leap forward. Of course, other humans with such capabilities might seek to use them for negative or personally profitable purposes. It was all the more vital to locate and assess them. Mac passed on that information to Tami Graves, who was deep in a national forest with Henderson and a group of the strongest Synons she had found in the area, practicing for a group attempt to reach Earth. Tami responded that this news was no surprise to her but was reassuring.

MacIntyre turned his mind to the paramount task of rescuing the child. Roger Singleton was perplexing. They must discover his motives and any other potentially dangerous activities. Vera Schechner had been right when she reported her research to him, describing Singleton as an enigma. Singleton seemed to be a visionary of high intellect and technical acuity, yet openly rejected climate change theories. Her suggestion that money was somehow involved had led Mac to deeper research in sources unavailable to Vera. He learned that Singleton's fortune and aristocratic heritage emerged from a centuries old coal mining family in England that had expanded to America; the enterprise still in operation and contributing considerably to his income. Singleton had a vested interest in fighting efforts to reduce carbon emissions. Coal was a major factor since it was mostly carbon that reacted with the air's oxygen to form carbon dioxide. Carbon dioxide was a leading cause of climate warming because it trapped heat in the atmosphere.

Mac chewed his lip. Singleton obviously needed a continuous inflow of money for his technical enterprises, as well as his lifestyle. He held many patents but had licensed only a few, keeping his innovations mostly within his own privately held company. What was he working on? All data pointed to robotics, a field that could involve myriad possibilities, both beneficial and alarming. There was scientific speculation that if and when any alien intelligence actually visited Earth, it would not be in biological form but machines. Robots could survive long voyages and hostile environments on worlds they explored.

Humankind's first forays into space exploration had been robotic crafts, a couple of which contained communications for any alien intelligence that might discover them. It was postulated that humans could eventually build intelligent robots. Mac thought of all the speculative fiction that abounded about intelligent, self-aware robots taking over the Earth. Indeed, if humans continued their environmental destruction, only machines would be able to survive. They required no oxygen rich atmosphere with protection from the sun's lethal heat, no water, shelter, or food. They would have no need, or perhaps appreciation of, a rich and varied animal and plant population. How would this benefit people? Some projected that a person's brain might be implanted in a machine, prolonging life in a new and indestructible form. Was this Singleton's vision? But why would that motivate kidnapping a child? A police detective's daughter.

An ominous thought crept in. Suppose Singleton had somehow learned of Emma's telepathic ability? Would he want to study her? How would that help him? Maybe he thought he might discover how to read others' minds, a useful tool in many situations. Mac needed Jeff to contact Emma again and find out exactly what Singleton had been doing with her. Had he asked questions? He immediately sent out a strong signal to Jeff.

■　■　■

Jeff had returned to his post and attempted to look engaged in his work, walking along his assigned veranda area, watching the guests closely. Suddenly, a voice invaded his mind, *Mac*, instructing him to find out everything Singleton had asked Emma or done to her. Jeff was flabbergasted that he could receive Mac telepathically from North Carolina. Maybe distance was irrelevant in thought transfer. He felt tingly, like he'd experienced a mild electrical shock—the force of Mac's power. No time to ponder the implications of his telepathic exchanges.

Jeff glanced up at the room on the third floor. The light was out. Someone had turned it off, apparently so Emma would sleep. He extended his mind, careful not to just stand transfixed as he had before, which might attract attention from nearby guards. He needed to be able to communicate with his mind while outwardly appearing to focus on his work. Long moments passed, frustrating him. Maybe the first contact had just been a fluke. Or maybe she could only do it awake.

He tried again. "Emma? It's Jeff. We talked earlier. I will help you, but I want you to tell me everything you can about what the people you're with have done or asked you."

Her voice whispered, faint but understandable. "They shot me with a needle. It hurt."

Jeff's mouth tightened with anger, recalling that she had previously said this. He paused for a moment, struggling to hide his emotion from the girl. He looked around. The crowd was thinning a bit. The pungent smell of salt wafted on a strong breeze from the Gulf, swaying table umbrellas and whipping ladies' skirts around. He got a grip on his fear of what Emma had endured—or would endure.

"And the shot make you sleep?"

"Yes. But they got mad. They wanted me to tell them about the fairies."

Jeff worked to narrow his focus and shift his personal thoughts away from those he sent Emma. He couldn't let her see how alarmed he was. He abruptly recalled the television interview that had brought Emma to fame, in which she babbled about fairies visiting her. Had that brought her to Singleton's attention?

These ruminations had taken only seconds but helped him to form his next question.

"They wanted to know about spaceships?"

"They think the fairies fly spaceships. My brother thinks that too."

"Did they say why they want the spaceship to come?"

"No. But they get real mad when I can't bring them."

An idea began to germinate. Jeff had to talk to Mac and the team.

"Have they said anything about tomorrow?"

"The mean man in charge told the other mean people to do whatever they had to."

"Tell them the fairies will come soon, but it will take a little while to get their spaceship here." Maybe that would stall them and protect Emma until the team could form and implement a rescue plan.

"You'll bring the spaceship?"

"Yes, I will. But tell them I need time to get it here. Tell them we know what they're doing and they better not hurt you. We will know it if they do. We can hurt them back real bad. Tell them your Fairy friend told you to say that but don't tell them my name. Let's keep that a secret between you and me."

＊　＊　＊

Jeff was anxious as he endured the tedious process of mustering out after Singleton's party had ended and the last guest escorted off the premises. There was a debriefing of all guards, then the temporary hires were separated and made to sign threatening nondisclosure agreements. They were individually searched, each piece of equipment and attire accounted for and confiscated. Then they were allowed to retrieve their clothing and personal belongings, paid in cash, and guided out by the permanent guards.

Once free of the compound walls Jeff knew what he had to do but was seized by mixed emotions: relief that he had survived the evening's ordeal, overlaid by an overwhelming feeling that he was abandoning a helpless child. He had to be patient, drive back to the secure communications at his trailer, and contact MacIntyre as soon as he got there. He was momentarily distracted by an urgent text from Suki notifying him that she was leaving Florida that night and to delete the burn-phone number she had been using while undercover in Naples. She would contact him soon. He hoped that she would succeed in safely getting away. She hadn't been able to tell him what she had encountered that night, but he suspected that she would be on Singleton's radar. Then, despite the late hour, he called MacIntyre.

CHAPTER ELEVEN

After Jeff helped her escape Singleton's home, Suki Kurosawa went back to her pricey short-term rental and began packing, planning to check out the next morning. She had to get away from the Naples circles she had been cultivating and their proximity to Singleton. They had served their purpose, and the image she'd carefully developed was ruined. Most important, Singleton was a danger to her. She should go straight home to New York.

Her phone rang. She rushed to answer it, expecting Jeff's voice, but instead heard sobs followed by words in Japanese. Suki sank onto the bed, stunned. One of her favorite uncles, a fisherman who had remained on the southeastern coast of Japan while other relatives immigrated to the United States, had been washed away by a sudden Pacific tsunami. Neither his fishing boat nor any crew had been found. Tears streamed down Suki's face as she recalled childhood visits with him and his family; his kindly visage floated in her memory. She found her voice and was thankful for having maintained fluency in her native language. She had to help her aunt, now left alone. She assured the older woman that she'd contact her parents, and they would work to get immigration status for her. Suki knew her father would do anything in his power for his widowed sister-in-law.

In the back of her mind ran dark currents. Immigration for her could be a complex process. Her aunt was a middle-aged woman with no skills and no knowledge of English; nevertheless, she tried to be positive in speaking with her. After hanging up, Suki sat thinking about all the stories she had seen and written about the many recent natural disasters. It bothered her, but until now had not triggered the kind of visceral personal reaction she was experiencing. Her mind's eye saw the globe covered with weeping people mourning the loss of loved ones, homes, jobs, and beloved locations. Was personally suffering its consequences the only thing that would make everyone wake up and do something about climate change? What an awful thought. She, as a journalist, could share her own experience, if she could find a media outlet for it. Perhaps the media should focus more on individual personal stories of loss. Should she reach out to her former employer, YCN? She resolved to contact their human-interest executive producer, Jack Harvey. Suki looked at the clock. Her parents were on the West Coast where it was earlier, but she forced herself to dial their number.

■　■　■

Manhattan seemed claustrophobic and dreary after Naples, Florida, but when the cab pulled onto her leafy upper west side street and stopped in front of her building, Suki Kurosawa felt a sense of lightness and joy. Once settled in, she tried contacting Jeff McCarthy. His phone number and email address were both disconnected. Not surprising. He was obviously undercover law enforcement. She searched the Web for his name and found only cursory information. She hoped he was safe. Above all, she wondered if they had been successful in rescuing Emma Goodsen. She reluctantly emailed Vera Schechner at YCN. Suki felt she had let down her former boss. She had little to submit from this costly freelance assignment other than an atmosphere piece about the local reactions to an assumed UFO sighting. What she had learned about Roger Singleton could not be shared publicly. There was no big scoop on the rescue of a kidnapped child. Suki felt like her connection with YCN would now be permanently severed. Her message to Vera was short. Suki wasn't in the mood for details right then. She would cobble together her video and written reports for their producers to salvage as best they could.

Vera Schechner's reply was terse. She had heard nothing from her contact and no information on the status of Emma Goodsen. The Florida UFO was relatively old news now. Perhaps they could do something with Suki's story on their website. Please submit the story and expense report. Expenses. Suki knew she couldn't submit all the costs she had incurred investigating Singleton. The apartment, clothes, entertainment. She'd just use them as unreimbursed expenses for tax deductions. She felt creeping depression. The Florida trip was time lost. She hadn't accepted offers that followed her departure from YCN and had sought no new assignments. There were no voicemails or emails for potential assignments. Her savings were quickly being depleted. She had risked assault and possible death for nothing. Exhausted and in despair she went to bed.

■　　■　　■

The jangling phone woke Suki Kurosawa as she slept in the next morning. Groggy, she lay in bed waiting for it to go to voicemail, then decided she should see who it was. The caller ID read "NSA." Suki grabbed the phone so quickly she almost dropped it. "Hello?"

"Ms. Kurosawa? This is Bailey MacIntyre. Jeff Hawke, McCarthy to you, worked with me in Florida."

His wording sent chills through her. "Is he okay?"

"Yes. Fine. And we've located Emma Goodsen."

"Oh." The word was couched in a long sigh, "I'm so relieved. Was I right?"

"Can't reveal details, but we appreciate your help. But you put yourself in jeopardy."

"Thanks to Jeff, I was able to get away quickly. I left Naples within hours."

"All good. However, Singleton has many tools available to locate people. He's probably already identified you through images from his security cameras. You need immediate protection."

Suki sat in a silent daze. How could she have not thought of that? And she had stupidly boarded a plane and returned to her apartment. "What should I do?" she murmured.

"He'll outsource to whomever he uses in New York. Someone should be ringing your doorbell any time now."

She felt panic rising. "What do I do?"

"It will be my person. Do you have an intercom or doorman?"

"Intercom."

"When it rings, just say the word 'who.' The reply you hear should be Mac's Deli. If it's anything else...is there a back way out of the building?"

She had put the phone on speaker and was dashing around gathering items and stuffing them into her carryon bag. "Yes, through the basement."

"Then hope they don't know about it. That will be your only chance other than going into a neighbor's apartment. It won't take long for them to get someone to open your door or break the locks. They'll be pros."

The jarring buzz of the intercom was so startling she almost tripped. "Did you hear it?" she whispered.

"Yes. I'll stay on the line."

Her breathing was so jagged she was barely able to utter the word, "Who?"

Her breath stopped for the instant it took to hear the answer, a male voice. "Mac's Deli."

Her breath rushed out as she replied, "MacIntyre's on the phone. I'm buzzing you in." Then to Mac, "Can you wait 'til he arrives? I'm still jittery. What if Singleton's people have tapped my phone?"

"It's not. Get your things. Follow my man's instructions. You'll be safe. I must go now. I have other urgent work to do."

Suki looked around her apartment, trying to calmly think of anything else she should take with her. She had her laptop and back-up hard drive. Most of her personal and work records were digital. A moment of sorrow swept over her. They'd probably break in and trash her home. It was a nightmare.

There was a light tap on the door. "Mac's Deli," the male voice said barely loud enough to hear. She slung her bag over one shoulder and her handbag over the other, grabbing the all-weather coat she'd thrown over a chair. Taking a deep breath she unlocked and opened the door. A handsome young man towered over her. "Hi. I'm Cal." He pushed his way in. "Is there a fuse box in the apartment?"

Mouth hanging open, she nodded toward the small kitchenette. He seemed to be there in two long strides, opened the fuse box door, and flipped the master switch. Then he was at the front door. "Is there a back way out?" Still tongue-tied, she nodded. "Be as quiet as possible. Lead me." He opened the door.

No neighbors were seen or heard; they easily took the elevator to the basement and exited through the heavy door which could only be opened without a key from the inside. "Give me your cell," Cal ordered. She mutely complied. He removed the SIM card, threw the phone on the ground, and smashed it with his foot.

"No!" Suki protested loudly.

He slapped a hand over her mouth. "Yeah, it cost you a lot of money." Then he gathered up the remnants and sprinkled them into a nearby dumpster. "Not worth your life if they use its GPS to locate you." She nodded sheepishly. At least he'd saved the SIM card.

* * *

Suki Kurosawa was comfortably and securely ensconced in a government safe house. She was becoming friends with her primary guardian, Cal Booker, who had rescued her. After he assured her of his security clearance and association with MacIntyre, she told him some of what had happened in Florida. He seemed to know more about it than she did but was reticent.

As she mused aloud to him about her uncle's tragic death in a Japanese tsunami, ideas began to form. "Do people have to personally suffer from the effects of climate change for them to take it seriously?"

"I think people let immediate concerns push aside the terrible things they see on TV."

"It made it real for me, losing my uncle like that." Her eyes glazed over. Then she said, "I have an idea."

Suki wrote up a proposal and sent it, not to Vera Schechner, News Director, but to Jack Harvey, who had created a successful niche producing what was referred to as "human interest" stories for YCN's varied cable, online, and streaming platforms. Her pitch was to research, interview, and submit pieces on individuals and families who had been personally impacted by a climate change disaster. Harvey quickly approved it. She would begin with her family's story.

■   ■   ■

Deep in an undisturbed forest, Tami, Henderson, Judilay, and Annilu met with a group of Synons living as humans in western North Carolina. Communing in their natural form without fear of being discovered was exhilarating. But they weren't on a pleasure trip. Tami's hope was that this large union of Synon minds could engage in a dialogue with Earth. Here, they were one with her glory on a narrow, winding river prancing over glittering rocks that also lined its banks, behind which the forest swayed.

Ancient emerald conifers stood sentry over leafy trees just beginning to show their autumn hues of gold, red, and orange. Wildlife crept closer, sensing the presence of their protectors. The sky was a deep azure. Tranquility prevailed.

After initial greetings, the Synons initiated serious discussions on how to best approach their mission. They didn't want to appear to be "ganging up" on their charge but needed to remind her that they were her intermediaries with The Living World, of which they were all integral components. Demonstrating this fusion, they spoke in a single voice, vibrating with power. They soothed, reassuring Earth that the Realm and The Living World weren't angry but concerned about her welfare and that of all the life she nourished. What could they do to help? As in prior encounters, the impression she conveyed was of severe illness that was provoking an immune response and resultant planetary imbalance. They saw that the source of her illness was clearly the planet's dominant species, which had grown invasive, eradicating large swaths of the ecosystems that guaranteed the sustenance of myriad interconnected life forms, destroying delicate balances in natural processes, and exhibiting selfish disregard for the consequences. The Synons asked how they could help her diminish her responses that were exacerbating the situation. The reply they got was the same as before with one vital exception. As each Synon heard "Only *they* can help," an image accompanied the words. As before, the communication was abruptly cut.

The sky splashed orange as Sol sank beneath the jagged mountain peaks. Nearly depleted of energy, the Synons agreed to rest for the night, imploring their natural surroundings to replenish them in their repose. As Sol appeared in the east casting a golden morning glow, the Synons roused refreshed and reinvigorated. They communed once more, each sharing with the others the image they had received. With reluctant good-byes, they floated away to resume their human personas and continue their work. Tami, Henderson, and their two Synon companions set out for the Tech Center. Their task was clear.

▪   ▪   ▪

As MacIntyre, Henderson, and Tami shared recent developments in the kidnapping of Emma Gooden, they began to see a multi-pronged path forward. They planned strategies and tactics that would call upon the full power of the Realm, and their own familiarity with human technology and imagination. Their considerable mental prowess was bent toward accessing, analyzing, and synthesizing factual, fictional, and folkloric data on the topic of alien spaceships. After an extensive dive into his background and biography, they made the extraordinary decision to include human tech center team member, Chris Mills.

▪   ▪   ▪

Standing in front of the closed door to MacIntyre's office, Chris inhaled deeply, trying to calm his jangly nerves. While MacIntyre and Henderson had always been cordial and respectful toward him and the other team members, he had exchanged few words with them directly. Now MacIntyre had called him into a private meeting, ordering him not to mention it to any teammates. Jeff had been gone for a while on some secret mission. Then the Synons had disappeared for a couple of days. What was going on? It had to have some connection to the startling news that had been shared with the team concerning efforts to contact the Earth in an effort to alleviate the spate of natural disasters. That had been the most mind-blowing revelation of his life. He was still trying to process it. What was he about to learn now? A long exhale, then he knocked on the door. MacIntyre's voice beckoned him to enter. As he opened the door he saw three Synon personas at the table: the familiar MacIntyre, Henderson, and the stunning Tami Graves. They all looked at him and smiled warmly.

"Come in, Chris." MacIntyre motioned to the fourth chair, which sat empty at the small table. Chris felt awkward as he sat his pudgy body in the chair. He brushed his long dirty blond ponytail from his shoulder, looking at the digital notebook he had just placed on the table, avoiding eye contact with the others.

MacIntyre attempted to put him at ease with a casual tone. "You know Henderson, and you met Tami at our initial meeting." His hand swept toward his two colleagues. Both smiled again at Chris. He glanced briefly at them, nodding. He tried not to dwell on the obvious fact that he was the only genuine human in the room. Would he ever be able to tell his grandkids about this? He smirked inwardly. Would he ever have grandkids?

Chris was an unconventional and eccentric physics major who was too undisciplined for academic or scientific life. Chris had always thought we could not possibly be alone in the universe and was fascinated by the possibilities posed by science fiction authors. He tried following his dad in the Air Force, hoping to worm his way into whatever might remain from Blue Book days. He and Jeff became friends when they were both selected for the same programs, disappointing for Chris, not of the Blue Book type. After his military stint, he wound up working with a think tank where Jeff found and recruited him for the Tech Center.

Tami's throaty voice filled the room. "We're fortunate to have you as a member of our little team, Chris." He had to look at her. He dipped his head, feeling slightly abashed. She continued without a beat. "We need your expertise for a vital mission."

Mission? Apprehension swept over him.

MacIntyre took up the narrative. "We need you to help us construct a spaceship that will convince someone highly knowledgeable in technology."

Chris had lost the thread at the words "construct a spaceship." His own voice croaked in his ears. "A model?"

"No." All three Synons answered in unison.

Henderson said, "A life-sized construction that can pass as a real alien ship." Chris merely sat with his mouth gaping. All three Synons burst into laughter.

Chris swallowed, forcing a chuckle. "Oh, so this is some kind of prank. Was Jeff behind it?"

Henderson's furrowed face grimaced. "Jeff is involved, but it's not a prank. You have the ability to help us. It's a serious matter. We know you've amassed a diverse collection of information on potential spacecraft, as well as designs from the imagination of writers, artists, and engineers. We need your expertise now."

Chris's next question was, "Does it have to fly?"

"Not if we can help it," Henderson drawled.

MacIntyre took over and succinctly explained to Chris Jeff's last conversation with the child, Emma, as well as what they knew of her kidnapper, Roger Singleton.

Mac's expression turned grim. "We need to rescue her as soon as we feasibly can. My sources tell me that her parents are frantic. The FBI controls the investigation, but her father, a police detective who's been ordered to stay off the case, is hounding them. Despite the fact that we now know Emma's location, we have no concrete evidence they could use to obtain a search warrant of Singleton's estate." Then he outlined the Synon's plan.

So, Chris thought, dumbfounded, it was about something more mundane than talking to Earth, just building a realistic spacecraft.

■　　■　　■

Emma awoke, the lingering vividness of the night's dreams more real than the morning light filtering through the heavy window drapes of the room where she was held. She stumbled off the couch where she slept and to one of the windows, pulling back a corner of the drape and peering down. Attendants were cleaning the wide veranda below, beyond which the Gulf of Mexico shimmered. There. She knew that was where he had been. She didn't know what he looked like, but his voice was clear in her mind. Her fairy friend Jeff. But she must keep his name a secret. She wondered if she could still talk to him, even if he wasn't standing below her window. She closed her eyes, concentrating on his voice.

The door opened and Luisa's call broke the spell. "Emma! Get away from that window!" The woman bustled toward her and Emma feared she would be struck, but Luisa's hands carried a tray. "Sit down there at the table and eat your breakfast right now. You have a busy day."

"Will the scary men be back?" Emma murmured, climbing onto the chair.

"They will indeed. And you'll fare much better with some food in your stomach, so eat up quickly."

"Can I go to the bathroom before they come?" Emma dug a fork into scrambled eggs. She was hungry but needed to use the toilet badly.

"Come on now, then." Luisa jerked her out of the chair.

Emma had ample time for breakfast, then sat on the edge of the upholstered chair Luisa had directed her to, her short legs dangling over its edge.

"Sit back and relax, now." Luisa said. She had brought in another smaller tray and set it across the room. Emma couldn't see what the things lying on it were. Emma obeyed, scooting back so that her legs were stretched out in the chair seat. Luisa took out a phone and spoke into it. "I'm ready, sir. Should I administer it now? Yes, sir. She's alert. Yes, sir." She put the phone in her pocket and approached Emma, stopping to stand over her. "Are you ready to tell the gentlemen what they need to know? I sincerely hope you are, because I don't know what will happen to you otherwise."

Emma looked up at her. "I have a message from my friend."

Luisa looked relieved. "The gentleman is on his way here. You can give it to him."

In a few minutes, the tall middle-aged man entered and strode straight to Emma's chair. Luisa had taken a seat on the sofa. She rose and spoke quietly to him. "Sir, she says she has a message from her friend."

Singleton dismissed Luisa. He wanted no one else to hear whatever the girl said. It could be childish gibberish, but he would take no chances. He looked down at Emma. "You have something to tell me?"

She looked back at him with unsettlingly intelligent eyes. "My friend has a message for you."

Singleton pulled an ottoman over and sat on it facing her, leaning forward on his knees. Who was her friend? He prepared himself for childish babble.

Her eyes were like knives boring into him. Her voice was low, almost a growl. "He says they know who you are and what you're doing and had better not hurt me because they can hurt you back real bad."

Singleton was stunned at the change in her demeanor. It was like a demon was speaking from within her. He shuddered involuntarily. Maybe it was. No, not a demon. An alien?

Singleton had a vision for the future that seemed inevitable. Machines would replace humans. It was just logic. He surmised it would happen in the near future, but beyond his biological lifespan. Unless other options appeared. Singleton was convinced that Earth was by no means the only repository of life in the universe; they were surely not alone in the galaxy. There seemed to have been too many reports over the decades of unexplained phenomena, popularly referred to as flying saucers inhabited by extraterrestrial aliens. Singleton thought that more than likely some were authentic, although probably not piloted by biological beings but by artificial intelligence or self-aware robots. He was intrigued by the potential of durable machines inhabited by the minds of former organic life forms. It would provide a means of achieving an expanded, perhaps immortal, existence.

Singleton maintained vast resources that monitored every mention of a possible UFO. Eventually, he would make contact. Wouldn't they value a human guide like him? There had even been recent reports of an Everglades sighting. If true, they might have landed nearby. Was this child somehow connected? He glared at her. "Is that all your friend said?"

She relaxed, confidence seeping into her posture. "No. They'll bring their spaceship. But it will take them some time to get it here."

Singleton tried not let his excitement show. The brat was smart, probably precocious. She could have concocted a story she thought he might want to hear. "How long?" He rose, looming over her. "I'm not a patient man."

"I don't know. But they said they'd know if you hurt me."

■　　■　　■

It took Chris some time to study various renderings of spaceships and draw up plans for the simplest ship that would most likely be able to fool Singleton, who was also well versed in UFO lore. It was difficult. There were so many possibilities. Traditional sightings of saucer-shaped crafts had formed the basis of many television and film spacecraft, but more recent fictional versions were usually more sophisticated and of varied shapes with exterior modules and paraphernalia beyond the early sleek depictions. Science fiction had incorporated the notion of huge "mother" ships, some cylindrical and long rather than round or elliptical. Of course, actual human spacecraft were small-crew modules, usually conical, not having ventured beyond the moon and more elaborate orbital space stations. Some designs for a proposed manned Mars mission showed a somewhat bullet shape consisting of crew and service modules. Since alien visitors would probably be way beyond the rocket propulsion that limited human space flight, their craft might well be beyond human imagination. They would potentially not carry biological entities but robots; or the ships themselves could be intelligent. They could be comprised of a unique biomechanical composition fused with intelligence. The question was: what would Singleton accept? He worked with robotics, so he might be comfortable with a more technically oriented intelligence. Too much time was passing while Chris and the Synons analyzed and discussed.

Finally in desperation Chris blurted, "Don't you guys know about alien civilizations, anyway? You oughta know what their ships are like."

The Synons smiled serenely at him, without mockery. Henderson said, "The Realm where we dwell is tethered to Earth, as are we. We communicate with The Living World, but Earth is our world."

"So can't you just ask The Living World what alien spaceships are like?"

The Synon turned to Tami Graves. She sat in thought a moment, then spoke softly, "People must learn for themselves, about their world, about other worlds. No person can know what is not yet ready to be known."

Chris leaned back, sighing. "I understand." There were many questions he wanted to ask, but these last responses had clearly indicated that he should never ask them. Even the most pertinent one: had Synons experienced any actual extraterrestrial visits to Earth? If so, they would be familiar with those spacecraft. Instead he simply asked, "So where does that leave us?"

"With Singleton. What will he accept?" Henderson said.

Mac began one of his elaborations. "My friend at YCN dug up some interesting background on him. His sparse public statements sometimes question human contribution to global warming and climate change. She dug deeper and discovered that his wealth comes from a long-held coal mining business in England, on his mother's side. It's still in profitable operation but under heavy scrutiny because of alleged environmental malpractice and a high rate of accidents and sickness among its workers. Protest groups are a constant presence. Singleton has no current management role, and his financial ties are intricately hidden. He speaks more often of his American business, robotics, and touts the bright future technology will bring. He might need money and be looking for new financial opportunities."

Chris felt more confident in speaking up now. "So he might speculate that extraterrestrial visitors would be mechanical rather than biological. And he could tap into their tech somehow."

Mac nodded, launching into another speech, directed at Chris. "I agree. Our ship could be a small, intelligent craft, perhaps with no crew." He hesitated. "But I've been thinking of more practical matters. Obviously, we haven't the time or materials to construct even the kind of spaceship mockup that a big budget film could. We deal in illusions. While Synons can transform ordinary matter into the semblance of something other than what it is, such as our own 'bodies'—he tweaked two fingers in the air—those 'objects'—another air tweak—don't have the mass and substance of the actual thing represented, although we seem as solid as a person. You can shove us and derive a sense of having pushed against mass, but these personas are our most complicated construct. We here have enhanced them considerably just since Tami learned so much about biology from her forays into the Internet and shared her findings with us." He paused and looked around the group. "Can we create a true facsimile of a spacecraft with enough mass and substance to appear real?"

Tami answered immediately. "Not if we have to transport it from where it's made to where we show it to Singleton. He has to come to the site where it's constructed."

Henderson took up the thought. "Then we need to build it in Florida, close to where he's holding Emma."

Mac smiled slyly. "I should be able to gain access to a small island off the Gulf coast. It even has an airstrip and a few hangars and living quarters." He saw Chris's mouth open with an impending question and put up his hand. "Don't ask." They all laughed. Mac's high security clearance and knack for networking provided him with a wide range of resources, none of which he would discuss. He looked at Chris. "Pack a bag and digitize all your material at once. And bring mosquito and sun repellent."

CHAPTER TWELVE

After a couple of days passed, Jeff was at loose ends, feeling out of the loop. Don't bug Mac. Don't whine. He kept telling himself. Then the phone rang.

Characteristically, Mac eschewed greetings. "Can you communicate with Emma again?"

Part of him was glad at the prospect of again being involved in the action, but Jeff felt like a leaf being buffeted around in the wind. "I don't know how close I need to be. I can try getting on the beach as close to the compound as possible. What should I say if I can contact her?"

"Go ahead and scout the area close to the compound, get some photos, but don't reach out to her, and don't allow yourself to be seen by the guards."

Sometimes Mac was insulting, but Jeff had to disregard it, remembering what Mac was. "Of course."

■   ■   ■

Singleton's compound was prohibited from blocking the beach in front of it to the public. However, jetties, ostensibly to prevent erosion, had been built at either end of Singleton's property, extending far onto the beach. Anyone could go around them, which could involve walking in water at high tide. Access to the beach itself was difficult because of the private property fronting it. Jeff had to park in a public lot and hike a considerable way down the beach until he recognized the massive structure he sought. It was a beautiful day, warm with a cooling breeze. He cautiously approached the jetty, stopped a bit short of it, and snapped a few shots of the compound configuration in relation to the beach. Then he dropped the beach towel he'd brought onto the sand and sat on it. The high wall extending from the end of the jetty to the building obscured the expansive veranda on which he'd stood as a guard. He could see the third-floor window behind which he was certain Emma was imprisoned. He longed to reach out to her. He forced himself to lie back and close his eyes. The sun was bright; he laid his cap over his sunglasses and dozed.

"Whadda you think you're doing?" a male voice boomed, jerking Jeff from a deep sleep in which he had seemed to be serenely floating. Disoriented, Jeff slowly moved the cap from his face and sat up. He peered up at a stocky, well-muscled man he didn't recognize, wearing a Singleton guard uniform. The man didn't seem to recognize him either.

Jeff fumbled for a story. "Uh, I was hiking on the beach and the sun just got to me. Had to sit down and rest, but I guess I fell asleep. I'm not trespassing am I?" He looked over at the jetty a few yards away.

"Close to it," the guard growled. "Better move on and find another place." He stood and watched Jeff awkwardly get up and gather his things.

Jeff nodded amiably to the guard. "Sure. You have a good day now." He loped off across the sand, feeling the guard's eyes on his retreating back. That was close. But at least he now had pictures of the beach in front of and next to the compound where Emma was, and, based on Suki's information, where Singleton's private area was.

He was still groggy, the dream state tugging at his mind.

Jeff's jangling phone forced him to focus. It was Mac. "Where are you?"

"Uh, on the beach near Singleton's."

"Has anybody seen you?"

He had to be honest. "I guess I dozed off on the sand. A guard I didn't recognize approached and asked me to move along." He waited like a child to be scolded.

"You sure he didn't recognize you?" Mac was surprisingly calm.

"Didn't seem to. As I said, I don't recall ever seeing him. He's probably day shift that I never came in contact with, especially if he patrols the beach."

"You haven't tried to contact Emma have you?"

Jeff was silent, experiencing a startling revelation. While sleeping he had dreamed that he was floating somewhere peaceful. His hand had been extended, holding another small one. Emma's. Emma floated next to him in the dream. They didn't speak. There was just quiet reassurance. "Jeff?" Mac's voice was urgent.

"Not consciously. I just now dreamed that she was floating next to me, holding hands. I don't know where we were. We didn't speak."

It was Mac's turn for a moment of silence. When he spoke his voice was gentle. "Jeff, you are a blessing." He gave Jeff no time to respond. "Before you get too far away, make another attempt to talk to Emma. Ask if she's alone, and if not, who's there. If someone's there, tell her to tell them her friend is contacting her and telling her what to say. If she's alone, just tell her what to say. She's precocious. She'll catch on."

"Okay. What do I tell her to say?"

"We are being hunted by the authorities and cannot risk leaving our secure hiding place. We will send an emissary to speak to her captors."

"That's too much for a girl her age. Even a smart one."

"Okay. Just say an emissary will arrive tonight."

"An emissary? Me?"

Mac chuckled. "You can't as yet give them the show they need. Tell them it will be tonight. Then go back to your trailer and relax. We have it under control."

Jeff was perplexed and resistant to again be put on the sidelines. "Hey, no. I need to know what's going on."

"Jeff, we can't risk anybody in Singleton's orbit connecting you. We'll see that you know what's happening. Also, I suggest that you exit the beach and return to your truck by walking on the street. Across from Singleton's. There's a sidewalk, isn't there?"

"Yeah. I guess you're right. I shouldn't cross Singleton's beach again."

■　　■　　■

Roger Singleton was a master of time management and mental compartmentalization. He didn't sit and fret waiting for Emma's next message. He went to his office and put his full attention on priorities. He surprised himself by jumping at the sound of his phone. It was his security chief. "Sir, one of the guards had an encounter just now that you should know about." Singleton was irritated at being interrupted but was curious enough to ask for a report. "One of the temps hired for last night's party was found sleeping on the beach near the northern jetty."

Singleton's irritation mounted. "Did he confront him?"

"He questioned why he was there, but he thought it wisest not to let the guy know he had been recognized. The guy said he was walking on the beach and got sleepy. He moved on when told to."

"So this guy doesn't know that he was recognized?" Singleton mused. His staff was accustomed to his silences. "Does he have a name?"

"Sorry, sir. He doesn't. He just remembers seeing this same guy working the veranda last night."

"Show him the ID photos of those who worked the veranda. Then do a deep dive on this beachcomber and report back to me."

"Right away, sir." Singleton had disconnected before this last acknowledgment was uttered. He swung around and gazed out at the secluded balcony off his office, considering the situation. Probably nothing of concern. The guy probably had noticed the nice beachfront and perhaps wanted to get a fuller view of the compound. It was impressive. Did he snap photos of it to show his friends to boast about where he had worked? That would be unfortunate. Well, he'd soon know all about him. His staff had access to extensive background check databases.

█   █   █

Jeff got as close as he dared to, keeping close to the upper part of the beach where palm trees and other vegetation, along with some walls and fences, provided a bit of cover. When he neared the jetties and no Singleton guards were in sight, he stopped and sat on the sand, closed his eyes, and attempted to return to the dream state in which he'd floated holding Emma's hand. It had never evaporated; he found it easy to slide back in. He concentrated on holding Emma's hand, then formed an image of her face in his mind and reached out.

At first he thought he was failing, but suddenly her voice reverberated softly in his head. "Mr. Jeff Fairy? Is that you?"

Relief and joy washed over him. "Yes, Emma. I'm staying near you. Are you alone?"

"No. Luisa is here but she's watching TV."

"OK. I need you to focus and listen very carefully."

"I will."

"Tell your captors that you have a new message from your friends. It's very important."

"I will. What do I tell them?"

"Have you ever heard the word 'emissary'?" He spelled it.

"No. Do I need to know it?"

Aware that she was advanced beyond other children her age, he felt comfortable. "Yes. Can you repeat it to me and then spell it?" He was amazed. She repeated it, then spelled it without hesitation. "Great, Emma. Now, here's what you need to do. Tell the bad people that your friends, remember not to say my name, have a new and important message. Here is the full message. They will send an emissary tonight. Now, let's practice. Repeat the message to me. She mentally spoke the words clearly and accurately spelled "emissary."

"Stay aware. It won't be long until something interesting happens. Soon after that you should be safely away from the bad people."

"Thank you Mr. Jeff Fairy! I'll do just what you say. Will I meet you soon?"

Jeff's heart melted. "Yes, you will." He hoped he was right.

      ▪   ▪   ▪

The matter of the suspicious guard moved to the back of Singleton's attention when Luisa knocked at his door. He was perplexed by the message she delivered. "Are you sure she said an emissary? That's a big word for a kid her age."

Luisa's big eyes reflected fear as she nodded vigorously. "Yes, sir. She said it slowly, pausing between each syllable. She even spelled it and made me repeat it to her."

Singleton's scalp crawled. Was this kid one of them? He tried to keep his discomfort from Luisa. "Tonight? An emissary will visit me tonight?"

"Yes, sir." She stood uncomfortably, waiting to be dismissed. He waved a hand at her as he picked up his phone with the other. She backed out, closing the door behind her.

Singleton ordered his security forces on high alert, rapidly deploying them throughout the compound, wielding automatic weapons. He seated himself on his private second floor balcony. It had no stairs to the veranda below and was only accessible by the French doors behind which his personal bodyguards stood.

He sipped brandy, watching the sun perform its daily light show, finally dropping into the Gulf's western horizon.

His security chief knocked, announcing himself. Singleton rose and went into the office. "Sir, I have information on the man on the beach."

■   ■   ■

Singleton again sat on his balcony, brandy in hand. He had quickly dismissed his security chief after learning that the temporary guard was an itinerant named Jeff McCarthy who had been asking about work along the Trail. He had passed initial muster with Parrish Ford and Pauley Moffit. He had moved around a lot, with few employers listed. An off-the-books gig worker with a couple of misdemeanor arrests without conviction. Nothing that raised an immediate flag; however, it looked like the kind of profile law enforcement might concoct for an undercover officer. He'd have his security guys drop in that night and interrogate him. They'd get the truth.

■   ■   ■

On the way to his truck, Jeff got a text from Bill, the local contact who had picked him up at the airport, with instructions to call him right away, which he did. Bill simply said, "Pack your stuff. I'll be there soon to get you and the equipment." Not long afterward, he had checked out and was following Bill's van to the same private airstrip where he had initially landed from Florida and was led to a parking spot. A plane a bit larger than the one that had brought him there sat on the tarmac. "Go ahead and make yourself comfy onboard," Bill told Jeff, tilting his head in the direction of the plane. "Take your own stuff with you. There's room for it."

Jeff grabbed his backpack and small duffel. "Okay. I guess there's no sense asking where I'm going." He grinned. All the way to the airstrip he had been speculating as to where Bill might be leading him. A degree of anticipation and excitement was building. He hoped he wasn't being shunted back to the Tech Center, when the Synons and Chris were obviously coming to Florida. He really wanted to experience whatever they had planned, and hopefully, participate in rescuing Emma. As he walked toward the plane, he was encouraged to see Bill unloading most of the electronic equipment that had been at Jeff's trailer and stowing it in the plane's cargo hold. Wherever he was going, it was going with him.

■　　■　　■

Singleton had returned to his office for a light dinner, then reclined in his luxurious chair, considering his extraordinary situation. Was this child truly in touch with extraterrestrials? He had made a calculated risk in orchestrating and implementing the girl's abduction. His most trusted operatives had been used. He was confident that their trail had been completely eradicated. The FBI, and any other law enforcement agencies involved in searching for her, would be working blindly. Nevertheless, the longer she was held the more vulnerable his position became. He couldn't stop now. He could be on the cusp of the most important event in human history, and he alone was in a position to fully take advantage of and control what would occur. He tried to tamp down anticipation.

A knock at his study door was followed by Pauley Moffit's voice. "Sir, do you have a minute?"

Singleton sat up in his chair anxiously, "By all means, come in." Pauley and Parrish Ford entered, wearing uncomfortable expressions. They stood, fidgeting. "Well? What did you get out of him?"

Ford swallowed loudly. "He's gone. Manager said he checked out this afternoon. He left in his pick-up with another guy in a van."

"Van? Wasn't the trailer furnished?" Singleton barked.

"I s'pose so. Manager didn't know nothing. He did say that the guy had added an antenna to his trailer. Figured it was for better TV than the campground provided."

Singleton cursed. The two men squirmed. "I knew it!" Singleton jumped up, full of frustrated energy. He paced, glaring at his employees. "Electronic equipment. What the hell was he doing? And who the hell is he?" He shot an angry look at the two men. "Go on, get out." They scuttled out, closing the door behind them.

Singleton's mind swirled. Could this mysterious Jeff McCarthy be working with the aliens? He shuddered as a more terrifying thought crept across his mind. Could McCarthy be an alien?

▪   ▪   ▪

As they lifted off, Jeff peered eagerly out the window. The flight was short. They never gained enough altitude for him not to recognize what they were flying over. When they approached the beach and headed out into the Gulf, he yelled at the pilot who, busy, wearing a headset, ignored him. Jeff wondered how the pilot could see at all with the setting sun like an orange spotlight filling the western sky; Jeff decided he should let him just fly the plane. Darkness had not fallen when they began descending. There was no land in sight back to the east, not even illumination from the shoreline. Suddenly, there was light below. They were landing on what looked like a tiny island.

       ◾   ◾   ◾

Roger Singleton dashed to the room being used to house Emma Goodsen, marched to the sleeping child, and shouted at her. "Is one of your friends called Jeff?"

The startled girl cringed and began crying. Singleton reached down and grabbed her shoulders, turning her to face him. "Who is Jeff?" he shouted. She looked up at him in terror, sobbing. "Quit sniveling and talk!" He glared down at the child. "Sit up!" he demanded. "Talk!"

Emma slowly sat up on the couch that served as her bed, covers sliding off to reveal her tiny body wearing the same shorts and shirt she had worn for days. Emma peered up at the big man, shoulders shaking. "He…he…said I shouldn't tell," she murmured, then broke out into new tears.

"So you do know this Jeff! Who is he? Is he an alien?"

Her voice trembled. "He's my friend. A fairy."

Singleton guffawed. "Fairy, yeah," he snarled. "How do you communicate with him?"

"He…he talks in my head."

Singleton jerked up the child and bore a finger into each of her ears. She howled. He stormed to the door, opened it, and yelled. "Did you morons check this kid for devices?"

Luisa emerged from Singleton's apartment at the end of the hall and almost ran, still holding the package of coffee she had been about to place in the coffee maker as she did each night. She arrived at the door panting and wide-eyed. "Oh, yes sir! The gentlemen made me do…nasty things looking for any hidden item for communication."

"And you found nothing?"

"No, sir!" Luisa looked pityingly at the sobbing child cowering in the corner of the couch. "Sir, she nor her mother knew she would be taken that day. Why would they have put such devices on her?"

"What about the things she had with her?"

"It was all checked thoroughly and discarded. Is there anything else, sir?"

"Get Pauley in here."

"Yes sir." She rushed away, bustling down the hall.

Singleton turned to Emma again. "Now tell me when this so-called emissary is coming?"

Whimpering, Emma's eyes were cast down at her hands twisting at the corner of the sheet. "He said tonight."

"Can you contact this Jeff again and ask him to be more specific?"

"I can try. What should I say to him?"

"Tell him my patience is running out."

Jeff was as excited as a kid when he emerged from the plane to be met by a grinning Chris Mills.

"Can you believe this?" Chris danced around. "Come on, I'll take you to your bunk."

"Good to see you. Is this some old military base?" They walked across the runway toward a cluster of flat-roofed concrete block buildings.

"I think so. Mac is closed-mouthed about it. It's the perfect place for us to work."

"What's going on?"

Chris's grin widened. "You'll see!"

They passed two buildings and Chris led Jeff into the third. "Nothing left here but bare necessities." He indicated the large, nearly empty room they entered. It held several tables with chairs. They looked like the utilitarian folding kinds available for various nonpermanent uses. At the back an open door provided a glimpse of a kitchen. Chris kept chattering. "At least we have private rooms." He led Jeff to the left down a hall lined with closed doors. "Bad news is that they're kinda like monks' cells." He opened a door midway down the corridor to reveal a tiny room with a single metal-framed bed against one wall. There was a small window; beneath it was a battered wooden desk with drawers on each side of a chair slid under its open center. In the corner behind the door was a metal rack for hanging clothes from which several metal coat hangers dangled.

"I've seen worse," Jeff chortled, dumping his bags on the bed. "Where's everybody else?"

"In the workroom. Next building over."

As they walked back through the open room Jeff asked, "Is that a kitchen? Any chance of getting something to eat? It's been hours since I had more than an energy bar."

Chris looked chagrined. "Oh, sorry. I should've thought about that. Yeah. I remembered to have food brought with us. Don't think they even thought of it. Let's get you a sandwich and coffee."

Carrying a wrapped sandwich in one hand and a lidded coffee cup in the other Jeff entered the workroom. Tami, Mac, Henderson, Judilay, and Annilu stood around a large round table looking at drawings spread all over it. They all turned and smiled at him. Chris, also carrying a sandwich and coffee, drawled, "Look what I found."

Tami spoke, still smiling. "So glad we got you out of there safely. Plus, we can use your input on our project."

"Good to see you all." Jeff sauntered over to the table, searching for somewhere to set his coffee. Chris dragged over a smaller table and a couple of chairs.

"Sit a minute and have your dinner," Tami said. "We can tell you what we're up to while you eat."

"Thanks." Jeff sank into a chair and dug into the sandwich.

Mac began explaining their plan. "We're constructing an alien spaceship for Singleton."

Jeff looked amazed and started to speak, but Mac went on talking, "We decided on the simplest craft, one that's fully automatic, no biological passengers. We think we can assemble it by tomorrow. We brought some materials with us. Chris provided a plethora of ideas."

Jeff dropped his sandwich on the table, stiffening in his chair. His eyes were glassy. Mac fell silent, as all present regarded him. "They're hurting her!" he exclaimed. He was silent again, deep in concentration, eyes still glazed. After a few moments, his eyes flew open. He spoke through clenched teeth. "Singleton's been roughing her up. Terrifying her. He wants to know what's holding us up and is losing patience."

Tami's eyes looked as if they were emitting sparks. "I'm doing my show tonight. That should buy us some time."

Jeff stared after her as she glided out, wishing he could see the "show."

CHAPTER THIRTEEN

Pauley Moffit assured Singleton that Emma had no access to communication devices. Singleton was still on edge. Night had fallen, and he asked that a snack and brandy be brought to the balcony off his study where he sat trying to relax and clear his head, although he was keyed up with anticipation. He ordered Pauley to call Luisa and inquire if the girl was asleep. No, he was told, she was just lying on the couch, covered with a sheet, wide awake, but still. A shudder ran through Singleton.

Time crept as a moonless darkness encroached. The only light was from a table lamp just beyond the door. The atmosphere around him abruptly seemed filled with electricity. Just in front of the balcony railing there seemed to be a disturbance in the air, a slight shimmer. He sat forward in his chair, peering into the darkness. Tiny sparks danced as the shimmer gradually coalesced into the shape of a woman. Singleton rose and stepped toward the apparition.

"No further!" a female voice reverberated.

Singleton could only stare at the figure, which had assumed some degree of substance but continued to shimmer. It resembled a woman but was far taller than any person he'd ever seen.

Wild silvery strands that were more like thin metallic wires than hair streamed out around the head, which was elongated and thin, dominated by huge, round, dark eyes. There was the slightest indication of nostrils and full lips that didn't move, even though the voice appeared to emanate from the phantasm. A hint of a willowy, well-proportioned female body appeared within a flowing expanse of silver material very much like that which crowned the head. It was both an alluring and terrifying spectacle. "Don't try to touch. You could instantly die," the voice intoned. "Did we achieve the correct human female anatomy?"

Singleton leered. "Oh yeah. And you've learned our language."

"We've monitored you for a long time. Perhaps our efforts to replicate your primitive bodies and speech will render you comfortable communicating with us. Now, I warn you. Keep your distance. What you see is but a projection, but its energy would be lethal to you."

He picked up an apple from the fruit bowl on the table and flung it. As it neared the figure it shuddered and fell to the floor.

"Are you encased in a force field?" He wanted her to know that he was knowledgeable.

"You might call it that. Now you waste valuable time."

He attempted bravado. "Why should I trust you?"

"It would be unwise not to. We need to see that the child is unharmed."

"Oh no. I won't fall for that trick. Where's the ship? Are you the leader? I need to speak to your leader. I can be of great assistance to you." He couldn't show weakness. He had to gain control.

"We do not understand the concept of leader. We will take you to the ship tomorrow, but the child must accompany us."

"What is the child to you?'

The voice became harsh. "You will not mistreat the child and will bring her tomorrow or face severe consequences."

Singleton was rattled but needed to demonstrate negotiation skills. "How do I know I'm not walking into a trap?" He noted that his prior question was not answered. Maybe the brat was one of them. He shivered.

"You are the one who wanted to see our ship. We know about you. We are willing to hear your proposal. You will obey us, however. Our powers so far exceed yours that you cannot comprehend them." Bolts of lightning rent the cloudless sky. A gust of wind hammered at Singleton, nearly toppling him. The table overturned, fruit rolling across the floor, brandy splashing as the bottle that contained it shattered.

Shaking, he struggled to regain his footing. "The child is fine," he squeaked.

"That is not what we perceived. You have mishandled her."

"No. No. I…just…shook her to wake her up, so I could ask when you'd be here."

"If she is harmed we will know. Immediately. You will suffer the consequences."

Singleton was visibly trembling. "I understand," he mumbled. "When tomorrow?"

"In the morning. We must ensure complete seclusion and security. When we are ready you will receive a text message. We are securing transportation for you and the girl."

She shimmered and disappeared, leaving behind a glowing energy field. Singleton sank into his chair and grabbed for the half-filled glass of brandy that had somehow remained standing on the table.

▪   ▪   ▪

TuMa'Aye Gra'vay, in her Tami Graves persona, had been busy reforming frayed connections among the multitude of earth-dwelling Synons. Many feared retribution from the Realm for having disappeared into their human personas, sometimes abandoning their mission. Many had remained in small groups, fearful that people would discover their nonhuman nature. Large numbers, however, had continued to toil at their mission, learning to skillfully navigate the two worlds of their existence, maintaining a delicate balance in their necessary interactions with people. Tami had initiated a cascading effort resulting in a widespread network that allowed not only for telepathy but also for quick and efficient identification of Passageways that could facilitate rapid movement between locations. Tami had taken advantage of this network to arrive on Roger Singleton's balcony in the form she had fashioned in which to greet him. She was pleased with the results of her performance. Now it was her colleagues' turn.

▪   ▪   ▪

Singleton spent a restless night. He rose with the sun and checked his mobile phone. No texts. He threw on clothes, stashing his phone in a pocket, and dashed out of his apartment, not bothering with his usual morning ritual of relaxing with coffee and digital newspapers. Luisa was just coming off the elevator to begin the morning's cleaning routine. He stopped her. "Get the kid cleaned up. Give her breakfast. Have her ready to travel at any time."

Luisa's eyes widened. "Should I say anything to her?"

"No!" He began striding toward the elevator then turned back. "Call the kitchen staff. I'm coming down to the dining room for breakfast." He needed to calm down and stay that way to be at his best for whatever the day would bring.

■   ■   ■

Another hurricane was marching across the Atlantic, gaining strength. The day on the small Gulf Coast island was blustery, with mist and occasional rain. Cloud cover would help cloak their illusion, but a storm could prove disastrous. They needed the helicopter to be able to pick up Singleton and Emma and then return Singleton to the coast. Then they would have to get Emma and themselves to a safer place as soon as possible.

The construction area buzzed. Jeff and Chris felt honored to be allowed to watch the five Synons work in their natural forms so they could direct all their strength to the task without having to maintain personas. Referring to the final drawing Chris had made, they utilized the materials they had brought, along with vegetation they had gathered from the island, fashioning what was gradually looking like a three-dimensional spacecraft. It was spherical, about six feet in diameter, with a matte metallic finish. They had decided not to use any element that resembled actual manmade space probes, satellites, or space stations. Extraterrestrials would have totally different equipment. They simply incorporated blister-like protrusions around the surface to simulate sensors. There was no "interior" since the craft itself was intelligent. No beings. They hoped Singleton would accept it. If not, getting Emma away from him was still their primary mission. However, learning something of Singleton's objectives was of high importance.

Time sped on, weather holding steady. When their work was completed the weary Synons withdrew to rest and supplement their energy. They had no idea what would be required of them. Tami, especially, needed to gather as much strength as possible, since she would again take on her role as emissary. Jeff and Chris, although exhausted, were too excited to rest. They raided the kitchen, sharing their excitement through mouths full of food and coffee. All too soon Judilay appeared. "Show time coming." He grinned. "The chopper just left."

■   ■   ■

The morning wore on. Dark clouds hung over the Gulf. Singleton tried to stay busy. He rehearsed what he would say to the aliens. Was he ready to give up the girl? It seemed to be a condition that they would not allow him to bring the girl back with him. Was this just some elaborate law enforcement scam to rescue her? No. How could anybody, other than his vetted and intimidated employees, possibly know he held her? If there was a leak it had to be this Jeff, whoever or whatever he was.

Singleton's thoughts were interrupted by a call from his security chief. "Sorry to bother you, sir, but I thought you'd want to know that we could find nothing on Kim Sawa."

"Find security cam footage of her and run it through the facial recognition program." Singleton hung up without a word, a habit familiar to his staff. He sat stewing. Was she involved? She had evaded his guards, leaving the compound swiftly after their encounter. Was she an alien too? She had obviously been snooping. Looking for the girl? His mind resumed its dash into paranoia. Should he alter his plans? Take the girl and go into hiding? He knew he couldn't. The aliens could find him. Besides, all this was just too enticing. If there was even the smallest chance that he was dealing with bona fide extraterrestrials he had to follow through. He tried to force himself to calm down, but the waiting was excruciating.

The buzzing of his phone woke the dozing Roger Singleton. Disoriented, he wondered idly how long he had slept. The phone buzzed again. He grabbed it, heart beginning to pound. A cryptic text message appeared, directing him to ascend to his rooftop helicopter pad, alone except for Emma Goodsen. Anyone who attempted to interfere would be terminated immediately. Hyperventilating, he called Luisa and ordered her to bring Emma to the elevator and wait for him. Then he called his security chief, ordering him to shut down the compound except for the elevator and alert the entire staff to remain in place and disregard any unusual activity, including the potential of helicopter traffic on the roof. They were to stay in that state until he notified them otherwise. After hanging up, a dark thought flitted through his mind. Should he make contingency plans in case he did not return? Shuddering, he dismissed the idea. He took a deep breath, visited the bathroom, washed his face, grabbed a jacket, then headed for the elevator.

* * *

Emma had been drifting in and out of sleep. She was frightened when Luisa woke her saying that she had to get right up. She almost dragged the girl from the couch and its rumpled bed linen. "Come on, Mr. Singleton doesn't like to be kept waiting." She took the little hand, leading her out of the room. Emma looked around. It had been days since she left that room and its adjoining bathroom. The hallway expanded before her. Luisa marched toward the elevator in which Emma had ridden the first day she was there. They stopped in front of its door.

"Where are we going?" Emma asked.

"I don't know. Just hush." Luisa glanced around anxiously.

"Is Jeff coming for me?"

Luisa peered down at the girl. "I don't know who that is or what Mr. Singleton wants. Just be quiet."

Emma reached out her mind. She was proud of herself. She was becoming good at it. She felt a faint presence. Jeff. She knew he was nearby. She grinned. Luisa looked down at her and made a sign to ward off evil spirits.

The tall mean man came out of one of the doors. He approached, scowling. "Luisa, you're dismissed for the rest of the day. Stay in your room. Obey Security." The elevator door opened and he pushed Emma in. She didn't like the sensation. It felt like part of her was staying and part was going up. Then the door opened, and he pushed her out. Wet wind slammed her face. It was cold. She shivered. They were in a big open space. The sky was all around except for the place where the elevator was. It was gray. She couldn't tell what time of day it was. They stood there for what seemed like a long time to her. Then she heard loud clattering and roaring. She slapped her hands over her ears. The wind whipped up around them. She was afraid it would blow her away. A big machine with long sticks whirling on top came out of the sky and sat near them. A door opened; Singleton growled, "Come on," and shoved her toward it. Terrified, she froze. He reached down and grabbed her like a parcel, ran to the door, threw her in, and crawled in beside her. "Let's go," he ordered.

A voice shouted, "Ear coverings in the seatback pouch." Singleton leaned forward and pulled out what looked like big earphones. He handed one to her. "Put it on for the noise." The machine began to rise. They were in what looked like a car's back seat. She glanced out the window in panic. Her stomach felt really funny. Quickly, they were moving out over the beach. She looked down and could see the waves lapping onto the shore. It was fun. It was like riding in a really fast car but they were up in the air. In moments there was nothing below except water. It was making her drowsy. She leaned back and fell asleep. Jeff was there, reassuring her.

· · ·

Singleton noted that they were going over the Gulf. Where was he being taken? The ride was bumpy; the wind was nearly too strong for a safe helicopter flight. He hoped it would not be a long one. His wish was granted. After a short time they banked, and he could see a small island below, landing lights guiding the pilot. It was afternoon yet looked like twilight under the heavy dark clouds. He was uneasy. Weather could quickly strand him here. As they landed, he saw that it looked like an old military base. Interesting. The pilot instructed him to alight and help the girl out. She sat with a beatific smile on her face. Singleton shuddered. He pulled her, dragging her out the door with him.

"You!" Singleton barked, ready to slug the young man who stood only feet away.

"Jeff!" The girl exclaimed; she ran to the young man who picked her up.

"Hello, Emma." Then he looked at Singleton with a mocking grin. "Follow me."

Singleton surveyed his surroundings as he walked. It was definitely a military installation. From the looks of it, inactive. There was a closed hangar and a few low concrete block buildings. He was led across a field overgrown with scrub. Ahead, he saw a tent similar to one that would be used as a field officer's lodging. Jeff stopped and nodded toward it. "Go on to the tent." Still holding the girl, Jeff turned toward the buildings. Okay, Singleton thought, I've relinquished my bargaining chip. With heightened senses and palpable anticipation, he hurried toward the tent, stopping in front of it. No sign of life. Should he go in?

A figure emerged. It was the female emissary. She looked more substantial than she had shimmering on his balcony in the dark. She held up her hand. "Halt there. I will explain." He stopped. She continued speaking, "As before, I am but an illusion constructed to provide you with a familiar figure with which to communicate. Within the tent, you will see my actual presence. I am not biological as you are. I am both machine and mind. Why do you want to confer with me?"

Singleton's fear had fled. He was inflamed with excitement. He found himself grinning. "Yes! Just what I anticipated. A robotic spacecraft. Do you know anything about me?"

"Yes. We have investigated you. We learned that you engage in a primitive form of what you call artificial intelligence."

Discouraged by the word "primitive" he quickly found his reason and voice. "I'm sure that in contrast to your advanced technology, my work might seem primitive, but for humans, it is quite superior and advanced. I am anxious to learn about you, but, primarily, I offer myself as a guide to aid you."

"You seem a fool. You have no knowledge of our intentions. Suppose our objective is to eliminate your species?"

Singleton was becoming accustomed to his body involuntarily shuddering. He knew that what this apparition said was logical, and possibly true. He struggled to keep his voice from trembling. "I understand. However, if that were your goal, you would not bother to converse with me. You'd simply eradicate us."

"Your thought patterns are undeveloped. Nevertheless, you speak with a small degree of logic. We are still in an exploratory mode. We came here to assess your evolutionary progress, which we see is stunted."

A pang of indignation for the human race prompted Singleton's response. "Perhaps your criteria is so different that you fail to appreciate how far we've come. I can help you comprehend." He paused. "Do you have a spacecraft within the tent? Might I see it?"

"We did agree. It is not merely what you call a spacecraft but my mentality and consciousness as well. Please step inside. I warn you that an attempt to touch it will result in severe discomfort, if not serious injury or death."

"I understand," Singleton replied. She stepped aside and he entered the tent. "This is it?" he muttered. So small and unimpressive. Yet, he thought, it appears to be a sentient craft, an extraordinary achievement. They do far surpass us. He walked around the spherical object that radiated a hint of energy. He turned toward the tent opening but did not see the emissary. Nevertheless he addressed her. "What is your propulsion system?"

She appeared just inside the tent opening. "As you would say, proprietary. At any rate, you could not in the least comprehend it."

He nodded. "Understood. Nevertheless, there are obviously vast differences between us. You cannot hope to grasp the nature of humans without a guide. I can be a conduit between our two species."

"Perhaps I am not a species." she stated flatly.

Again the involuntary shudder. "It's just a term we use based on how life has evolved here. It only illustrates the degree to which you need an interpreter."

She laughed harshly. "We know more about you than you are capable of ever learning about us. We need no guide or interpreter. Your communications methods are so primitive and simple. Everything about your society is simple, albeit contradictory."

Singleton was becoming desperate. He had to learn about these entities, acquiring enough of their technology to apply it to his own work and gain dominance. He tried another approach.

"I am in the vanguard of human intelligence. If I could utilize but a tiny fraction of your technical superiority, I would lift my species beyond their animal instincts to attain mental clarity, leave behind their squabbling and greed, all the traits that make them dangerous to this and other worlds."

"You make something of a point. If your species continues on its current track you will destroy yourselves and your own world. We see that you aspire to colonizing other worlds in the future. That could not be allowed if you merely advance technically and not mentally. Your chemical reactions, which you call emotions, make you volatile and reckless."

"Yes!" Singleton agreed as if he were not a member of the species being described. "We need you to teach us. I would be so honored to—"

"Enough! You must return to your home before the threatening storm arrives. Please return to the waiting helicopter at once." She stepped away from the tent opening.

"Will you contact me after you—"

"Cease your gibberish. Board the waiting craft." Her voice had taken on a quality of command that sent Singleton dashing to the helicopter. The pilot motioned him to duck under the whirling blades and get in. Before he could get his safety belt fastened they had lifted off.

Singleton glanced back down at the island. If the emissary was truthful about its own nature, the people he saw scurrying about were, in fact, human. That was disconcerting. The aliens already had human partners. Perhaps he should have tried befriending them in an effort to join the group. There was one more possibility. He needed to talk to Kim Sawa.

CHAPTER FOURTEEN

Jeff carried Emma into the common room and sat in a chair, holding her in his lap, hugging her tightly. He spoke soothingly. "You're safe now, Emma. It's going to be night soon. We'll go somewhere safe from the storm, and tomorrow you'll go home to your family."

"Will I get to see other fairies?" she asked gazing up at him.

He grinned as an idea took hold. "Yes. You will." He sent a telepathic message to Lewis Henderson. "Nap a bit now." She snuggled into his chest and fell asleep.

■　■　■

The hurricane that was ravaging Central America produced wide-reaching bands of rain and wind that approached south Florida. The helicopter pilot had been instructed to return to his base on the mainland after dropping off Singleton. Now the handful of people and Synons on the island were securing it and preparing to leave in the plane that had brought them there. The tent was dismantled and returned to its storage area. The "space-craft" was simply allowed to collapse into a pile of vegetation and scrap metal. The vegetation was spread across the field while the larger items were stowed in the plane's cargo hold to be recycled or disposed of later.

Jeff had taken Emma with him to his tiny room to get his gear. Seeing her shiver in her skimpy clothes, he wrapped a shirt around her and tied the sleeves together in the front. He hefted his gear and the child, talking to her in a way that he realized was similar to his verbal addresses to Cosmos. Just as they entered the common room, the front door opened, and sparkles dancing in the air approached them. "Look, Emma. What is that?" Jeff murmured. The sparkles coalesced into a tiny female figure, with long blond hair streaming down to touch delicately flapping gossamer wings. Sparkles twinkled around her. Emma's eyes grew huge. "A real, live fairy!" She tried to jump out of Jeff's arms, but he held her tightly.

"You shouldn't touch her. She's so tiny you might hurt her." Emma stopped struggling.

The fairy spoke in a soft musical voice, "Hello, Emma. Now I and my friends will take care of you until you are back with your family. We must go now. It will storm soon." She turned and flew back out the door, disappearing in the falling darkness.

"A real, live fairy! A real, live fairy!" Emma sang. Jeff struggled to keep her still, as he carried her to the waiting plane.

■　　■　　■

As Emma slept soundly, strapped into her seat, the Synons and men discussed the mission.

"Singleton clearly was after whatever alien technology he could snag," Tami said.

"Did he really buy our extraterrestrial sham?" Chris asked.

Lew answered, "I think he truly has convinced himself that aliens are visiting Earth, and so he was ready to accept us. His greed led him to see what he wanted to. He's dangerous. He'll obviously work with anybody he thinks can give his business an edge."

"Unfortunately, he didn't commit a crime," Mac mused.

"What about kidnapping Emma!" Jeff exclaimed.

"The manner in which we rescued her let him off the hook."

"Why didn't you arrest him instead of letting him go?" Jeff was indignant.

"We have no proof on which to arrest him. He had the child but could have said he found her wandering the streets. In order to prosecute him, we would have to disclose our own actions, which we obviously can't do. Her testimony would be questionable. She's too young."

"So he gets away with it. No consequences at all. That just doesn't seem right." Chris was as upset as Jeff.

Tami spoke. "We could have tipped off the FBI to her location. But we had no way of providing them with evidence, not even enough for a search warrant. It's a conundrum we Synons live with."

"I'm not a Synon," Jeff growled. "I should have done something when I realized where she was. If I could have seen her, at least they'd have my testimony."

"No they wouldn't," Mac said soberly. "You'd be dead."

Jeff sat stewing.

Chris spoke softly to him. "You know how many guards he had. You'd never have made it to the second floor."

"Suki did. I could have told them Singleton sent me on an errand."

"They'd've caught and restrained you. They would interrogate you in a very unpleasant manner. You wouldn't talk, so Singleton would have you 'disappeared.' You'd be dead."

Tami said, "Suki's situation was different. Singleton took her to the second floor. He probably sent guards away thinking he could easily handle her alone. She proved more than he anticipated. But she was lucky to get away when she did."

"We'll keep him under surveillance. He'll slip up somewhere," Mac said reassuringly.

Jeff peered at Mac. "So how do you handle the press, even her family, when Emma's returned? I guess you have a story."

Mac responded, "I'd like to contact Mr. Goodsen and meet him alone to explain that we discovered her as part of an ongoing classified investigation and no further information can be released. He'll understand since he's a police detective. It will rattle Singleton." He chuckled. "He'll be squirming, wondering whether the extraterrestrials will contact him or not. I fully intend to dig deep into any government contracts he might have. I'd like to find ways to cut him off entirely. I'm not done with him by a long shot."

Chris changed the subject. "So where are we going? Why can't we just take her home tonight?"

Mac responded, "We're all too exhausted to properly handle it tonight. We'll spend the night in Central Florida. I've made arrangements."

Emma, sleeping in Jeff's lap, head snuggled against his chest, awoke when the lull of motion ended, as the car stopped at the motel. It was late, but the vintage neon sign's vibrance lit the night. The sign bore vivid green and hot pink letters reading "Flamingo Family Motel" above a tall, intricately designed flamingo in all its glorious color. The building illuminated behind it was painted a bright pink with green trim, the total image recalling Florida's twentieth century Art Deco heyday.

Mac had booked the entire place for the night. The occupants of the two vehicles wearily trudged into individual rooms, which were clean, updated, and attractive. Tami tried to coax Emma into her room, but the girl wouldn't leave Jeff. "I'll tire her out, and then maybe you can bathe her and get her to bed," Jeff suggested. "We both are fascinated by the little waterfall visible through my window. In fact, she's demanding to go out there tonight." He pointed to a cascade in the creek that ran behind the building. It was artfully lit by strings of tiny white lights that made the water appear to be dancing. A curved walkway led from the paved sidewalk along the back of the motel to the creek bank, along which sat benches and a picnic table.

"Pretty," Tami mused. "Just don't let her tumble in. And be quick. I'm exhausted. Just knock on my door or ring my room when you're ready."

As tired as she was, Emma was exhilarated by the prospect of visiting the waterfall and creek. Jeff felt a surge of energy and anticipation. They exited through the front door and she ran behind the building and down the path to the water. As he strode along beside her, he was aware of a fresh crispness in the air. A panoply of twinkling stars above seemed to mirror the light prancing on the water's surface. A palpable sense of belonging swathed Jeff in serenity. He caught Emma's hand as she approached the creek bank, which he saw was lined with green wrought iron fencing, low enough to be unobtrusive but high enough to stop a capering child. Emma skidded to a halt, giggling. She looked up at him with joy. As they smiled at one another, Jeff felt the same kind of tickling sensation in his mind that he had felt the first time Emma mentally contacted him. Her eyes widened. The water rippled. He felt a distinct presence embracing him, but no one else was visible. He was shrouded in love. It emanated from Emma but also from the water, the trees and vegetation, the stars, the breeze. Emma was staring intently into the water; he followed her gaze. A faint light shimmered below the current. Abruptly, Jeff knew what it was. Basking in newborn emotions, he whispered, "Thank you. Make me understand what I can do, what all of us can do, to help you."

"More of us," Emma's tiny voice tinkled. "She needs more of us."

The Synons, in repose in the seclusion of their rooms, simultaneously felt the contact and reached for one another in elation. It had happened! They now saw the path ahead.

■　　■　　■

As quickly as Earth had joined them she withdrew. Jeff and Emma stood still and silent for long moments, gazing into the water. Peaceful exhaustion washed over Jeff. He glanced down and saw the child's head nodding. Swooping her up in his arms he murmured, "We are fortunate and will act on her wish, in time. Right now, you need a warm bath and bed. Let's visit Tami."

When they reached the building front, the door to Tami's room stood open, light spilling out revealing the others of her kind and a disheveled Chris within, all wearing wide grins. Tami drew Jeff and Emma into a quick embrace. "We are blessed," she whispered. When they had entered her room and shut the door, Jeff felt that they could have turned out the light and still be illuminated by the gathered Synons.

Noticing that Emma had fallen asleep in Jeff's arms, Tami murmured, "Bath has to wait 'til morning. Jeff, do you mind if she sleeps in the second bed in your room? I sorely need my Synon privacy tonight."

"Sure," he said. "I'm about to conk out on my feet. I'll set an alarm. Then we can all enjoy the night. The best night of my life; well, a close second was the one when Cosmos contrived to bring Marie and me together the way we should be, with him in the middle, of course." He grinned widely.

Overwhelming awe kept Jeff awake. Awe and reckoning. Somehow, he had been drawn into this series of events that now set him, along with a young child, in a place beyond everyone else. Earth had communicated with him and given him an order.

Since his first encounter with Tami Graves Jeff had felt that he had lost his ability to be proactive. He felt passive and filled with resentment because of it. Maybe there were times when a person had to accept being led along until their path became clear. Now he had an objective that would require multiple steps to reach. Many small goals to accomplish. He felt empowered. He would make choices, but in concert with those on whom he must rely as allies to complete his mission. Purpose coursed through him, and then he was claimed by restful sleep.

•   •   •

The group recognized Emma's unique intelligence, but were, nevertheless, concerned that she would, in a moment of childish excitement, talk about her experiences in captivity, as well as with telepathy and the mysterious people who had rescued her. They attempted to explain to her that these secrets could never be revealed to others. It could cause great harm to her friends.

"You had some strange dreams." Jeff sat across from the child, leaning forward on his knees to look at her. "You dreamed you were in a strange room in a strange house, and mean people talked harshly to you and gave you shots, didn't you?"

"Yes! That was all dreaming?"

"It was."

"How do you know all that?"

"It's part of my job to protect you. Besides, you know we can visit your dreams. Sometimes we just remain silent when it's the best thing for you. You must never speak of those dreams to anyone other than me and the friends with us now. Speaking of any of this could cause harm."

"I can keep secrets." Emma smiled slyly. She lowered her head. "When you take me home will you still be near me?"

"Jeff suddenly recognized what the term "heart wrenching" meant. "We live a long way from you, but we can still visit in dreams."

"I'll tell Mommy and Daddy I want to visit you!"

"I'll always be your friend," he croaked. He hoped she wouldn't make a scene of clinging to him when it was time to leave. He knew her detective father might be suspicious of her attachment to this strange man. Hopefully, Mac's cover story would reassure her parents.

■ ■ ■

It was a Saturday morning. Mac telephoned Emma's home early, hoping to catch her father.

It rang several times, then went to a voicemail greeting in a male voice that provided no identification, simply an instruction to leave a message.

"Mr. and Mrs. Goodsen, I'm Bailey MacIntyre. You should see a National Security Agency identification on the phone number I'm calling from. I have good news for you regarding—"

"Hello," a man's voice broke in. "Be reminded that I'm a police officer, so if this is a scam you're in trouble."

"I understand your caution. It's smart. Is this Mr. Gary Goodsen?"

"Yes. Who are you?"

"Bailey MacIntyre. I am with the NSA. Check your caller ID for verification."

"Just a second. I have to put you on hold to check it." Shortly, Gary came back on the line. "OK. I'll accept that you're NSA, but I'm aware this could be a spoofed number."

MacIntyre ignored the comment, launching into his speech. "Please listen carefully. In the course of an ongoing classified joint agency operation, we were fortunate to stumble upon the location of your daughter, Emma."

"Emma! Is she alive?" In the background Mac heard a woman's excited voice. "Wait, Nina," Gary said sharply.

"She's not only alive, but we have her with us and can bring her to you shortly. We have a few requirements, however, for security purposes."

Gary's voice sounded skeptical. "Look. We've had enough wackos and con artists—"

Mac interrupted, in a natural tone and volume but infused with his Synon voice of command. "We're who I say. And you're wasting time." There was no response, so he continued. "You must keep publicity at a minimum. As I said, she was found during an investigation that touches on national security that cannot be revealed in any form. Get paper and write this down. I'll wait."

"I have paper here." Gary's voice had taken on the same neutral professionalism as Mac's.

"This will be the only press statement you ever make. Write it down: 'Our missing daughter has been safely returned to her home. She was rescued during a classified operation conducted by joint law enforcement agencies. Since the mission is ongoing, no details can be released for the safety of those involved and the integrity of the mission. Please do not ask questions. They cannot be answered.' Got that?"

"Still writing."

Mac waited in silence a few more moments, then Gary Goodsen said, "I suppose you know our address?"

"Yes. Is an hour from now good for you?"

"Of course!"

"Mr. Goodsen, you must impress upon your wife and son the necessity for confidentiality. Lives will be in jeopardy if there is idle talk or speculation. Your teen son, especially, must be ordered not to mention this in any way. No social media posts or comments. No emails. No chatter on websites or to any reporters or members of the public, including his friends."

"I'll ensure that. My family understands how loose words can endanger law enforcement officers. It's been drilled into them. I'll reinforce this order."

"One hour, then?"

"One hour too long, but come on." Gary's tone had become almost friendly.

■　■　■

"Emma!" Her family called her name in unison, as they rushed toward her. She stood just inside their front door, which Mac had quickly closed behind himself and Jeff. They stood on either side of the girl. Emma looked confused momentarily, then scuttled toward her family. Gary grabbed her up while Nina and Liam jostled to hug her, all talking at once. Gary, always able to maintain steadiness, said with a laugh, "We'll smother her! Come on, let's sit down." He strode to a couch and sat in the middle, arranging Emma on his lap. Nina, weeping with joy, and Liam gathered close on each side of them. A sudden hush fell.

Jeff felt awkward watching the tableau, aware of the sense of loss coursing through him. Emma gazed at him, pointing. "That's my friend Jeff!"

Attempting to sound professional he said, "Jeff Hawke. This is my NSA colleague Bailey MacIntyre, who called you." Jeff realized he'd insinuated that he was also NSA, but maybe that was best in the situation.

Nina gushed, "We can never thank you enough!" As if some inward mechanism jolted her into hostess mode, she added, "Please sit down. Can I get you some refreshment?"

Both men took seats on the facing couch. Bailey spoke kindly. "Thank you, Mrs. Goodsen, but we're fine and can only stay a few minutes. We have a plane to catch." He looked piercingly at the group across from him, assuming an authoritative tone. "I suppose Mr. Goodsen has impressed upon you the absolute urgency for all of you to maintain confidentiality in this matter. I provided him with a short statement for the press. It must be the only words ever spoken or written about this situation." He looked straight at Liam who squirmed. "Liam, you are a teen, and as such I know you are used to sharing your experiences with friends in person, online, and in any way possible, but your father assured me that as the son of a police detective you fully comprehend the dangers of revealing anything about ongoing investigations." He looked at Nina. "You as well, Mrs. Goodsen. As an adult you have more inherent self-control, but you cannot feel that you can confide in just one person, like a relative, best friend, or even clergy. Do not allow wheedling acquaintances to unlock your lips. This is a very sensitive situation. I reiterate that lives are at stake along with potential matters of national security."

Delighted that this NSA agent had called him a teen, Liam had been mumbling, "Yes sir. I understand," as Mac talked over him to his mother. Nina nodded emphatically. "You can be assured that the Goodsens will not speak or write any words beyond those dictated to Gary. We do fully comprehend the potential consequences." Gary beamed with pride.

Jeff sat with his head down, hands dangling between his knees, fighting an urge to giggle. Mac sometimes treated people as if they were idiots, but he understood the need for emphasis and reinforcement. The Goodsens didn't seem insulted. Had they not been a law enforcement family, it might have been quite different.

Emma piped up, "I won't say a word!" Laughter broke the strained mood. The girl seemed to search the room with her eyes. "Where's Fuzzy?" She seemed slightly worried.

Liam replied with a wide grin, "Sleeping on your bed. Where else?" He caught Mac's sharp glance as he inclined his head toward the back of the house. Liam nodded. "Let's go see her." He stood, helping his sister to stand, holding her hand as he led her off.

Nina watched them go, still tearful, but smiling. "She adores that cat," she murmured.

Mac took that opportunity to continue his lecture. "Emma has been checked medically and doesn't seem to have been harmed. She appears to have been kept sedated for the most part, with a mild enough drug to allow dreams, about which she babbled to us. We told her to not talk about them to you or anyone. The doctors think that's the best way for her young mind to process it all. It will fade into a jumble of dreams and be forgotten. Speaking of it will only serve to keep the dream memories alive. Parents naturally need to share their children's experiences and help with the coping process, but in this case, that would have an opposite, detrimental effect. You must act like nothing happened. She'll quickly readjust to the routine of her life. Please don't send her to school for a while. Nowhere that other children or adults will ask prying questions."

"She's going into first grade," Nina said with concern. "We don't want to hold her back. She's intellectually ahead of other children her age."

"We quickly learned that." Mac smiled. "She'll be in a position to skip a grade or enter a special program for gifted children. She'll easily catch up." He paused. "In fact, we're familiar with a well-regarded summer camp that provides individual tutoring for advanced students, as well as traditional camp activities. You might consider sending her there next year. It would be like a vacation for her, and she would meet other precocious children. I can get you information on it."

Jeff shot him a questioning look but kept silent. He didn't want to jinx whatever scheme Mac was hatching.

Mac kept talking. "When she's back to a normal routine you might consider sending her for a short visit to this camp."

The Goodsens' faces had darkened. Gary said tersely, "I'm not so sure of that. She's too young to send away alone, even for just a summer."

"And after this ordeal," Nina interjected softly, "we want to keep her close. For a long time."

"Understandable." Mac nodded. "I agree with you, Mrs. Goodsen. But within a year she'll possibly become bored and in need of a more advanced education than available here even in the best of schools."

"Where is this place you're pushing?" Gary said suspiciously. "I'd like to look it up."

"They don't advertise and maintain a low profile. Admission is by appointment or recommendation only. Usually from graduates or their families."

"Sounds kind of fishy to me," Gary growled.

Mac laughed. Jeff forced a grin. Mac retorted smoothly, "We are in the business of fishy, Mr. Goodsen. Many government officials and academics send their children there. I'll have a brochure sent to you that contains references you can contact."

"That doesn't mean a damn thing," Gary exclaimed. "The references could be planted. Don't try to jerk me around. And while you're at it, could I see that NSA badge again?"

Jeff was torn between insult and mirth. This guy was a match for Mac. No wonder his daughter was so clever.

Mac calmly pulled out his badge and handed it over to Gary. "You can take down this identification number and contact NSA to ask if it's authentic and is assigned to my name. I work in high security areas, so they can't give you any information on me other than verification of my affiliation with them." He grinned again. Jeff couldn't recall ever having seen him grin so often. "I can see where Emma gets her smarts. I think your department is fortunate to have you as a detective."

Gary looked somewhat sheepish as he returned the badge. "No offense, sir. I've done my time investigating scams and cons. And I'm protective of my family."

Nina burst into loud sobs. "It's all my fault," she wailed. "I should never have let her go to that woman's home without making sure I knew where it was and had an accurate phone number." Her head sank into her hands as her body shook.

Gary's arm swiftly went around her. "No, no, honey. These were obviously real pros. Neither my department nor the state police have been able to find any trace of who that woman was." He looked at Mac and Jeff. "Maybe the FBI?"

Jeff knew to keep his mouth shut. Mac answered, "Even to you, as fellow law enforcement, I can't comment. However, as

I said, she was located during the course of an ongoing investigation by a joint task force. You're right, the kidnappers were professionals."

"But why Emma?" Nina sobbed.

"We don't know." Mac said flatly. "If we learn anything that can be confidentially revealed to you, we'll do so. You need to put it behind you. She's safe now."

"And she'll stay that way," Gary added. "I'll see to that."

Mac just nodded, then rose to his feet. "We must go."

Jeff took that as an order to also rise. But he was reluctant to leave. He looked at Mac. "Is there time to say good-bye to Emma?"

"I'll get her." Nina jumped up and hastened to Emma's room.

Mac smiled again. Jeff wondered how many times so far. "We need to be quick." He regarded Gary, who also had stood. "It was Jeff who took control of Emma after her rescue. Even though a female colleague cared for her, Emma became attached to Jeff."

Nina returned with her two children in tow, followed by a big orange tabby cat. She looked down at Emma. "Honey, your friends have to go now. Thank them."

"No! You can't leave!" She dashed to Jeff wrapping her arms around his legs.

Endeavoring not to burst into tears, he gently unwound her arms and knelt, holding her hands in his. "Emma, I must go to my own family now." Fuzzy was nuzzling Jeff, rubbing his head against him. Jeff released one of Emma's hands and gently petted the purring cat. "I have a cat at home that misses me the way Fuzzy missed you. I should go see him."

"Can I visit you and meet your cat?" Tears were streaming down Emma's face.

"Uh." Jeff was at a loss for words.

"Maybe we'll take a trip to see Jeff and his cat," Gary said huskily. "Where do you live, Jeff?"

Mac interjected, "North Carolina, mountains. You'd enjoy it there."

Gary guffawed. "We were there not too long ago. Beautiful country, but our vacation was cut short by a fire, storm, and an earthquake. You live in a pretty dangerous place."

"That was a freak of climate change," Jeff said quickly. "Very rare. Weird even."

"Daddy, can we go? Can we?" Emma pleaded.

"Maybe in a bit, honey. I think Jeff will be busy a while." He looked at Jeff, reaching into his pocket. "Here's my card. It has my personal email address on the back. Keep in touch."

Taking the card Jeff said quietly, "Thank you, sir. I will."

Mac was opening the front door. He nodded at the Goodsens. Liam had joined them and all were speaking "thank you" at once. As he went out the door Jeff sent a mental message to the child who stood weeping in front of her family. "If you need me you know how to reach me." They grinned at each other.

■　　■　　■

Chris and the Synons had arrived back at the Tech Center beset with weariness. The Synons were in dire need of privacy to rest and replenish. Chris was so tired he practically stumbled, but his mind was so wound up he didn't think he could sleep.

Before respite, however, they were surrounded by those who had remained at the center, all talking at once.

When Judilay saw Lana he impulsively hugged her. "It's so good to see you!" he murmured, surprised by the unexpected warmth and substance of his "body" against hers. She allowed the embrace to linger until he released her with a grin. "I've got a story to tell you!" He laughed. In the general confusion, no one noticed the exchange except Tami Graves, who was disturbed by what she had witnessed. As she considered the need for a private talk with Judilay, Tami realized that training programs should be devised to help Synons navigate relationships with humans.

Forcing her attention away, Tami found the strength to raise her voice. "We'll fill you in tomorrow. We're all in a state of exhaustion now and must have immediate rest."

Lew Henderson took control. "Tami's so right. All of you take the rest of the day off, and get out of here as soon as possible. We need to rest here for a while before going home."

Marie jumped into the moment of silence. "Where's Jeff?" She looked alarmed.

Lew patted her shoulder in a fatherly manner. "He and Mac stayed to return Emma Goodsen to her home." A loud murmur arose. "Yes, yes. She's safe. Long story. Tomorrow. By then Jeff and Mac should be back, if not this afternoon or tonight."

The look of relief on Marie's face put a big grin on Lew's.

■　　■　　■

Jeff and Mac were the sole passengers on Mac's small plane, which had been flown to a local military airfield to pick them up.

Jeff was pensive. Mac broke the silence. "You and Emma formed a strong bond through your unique abilities. She's young and will bounce back into her life. At her age, it's not even certain that she'll form permanent memories of these recent events. For you, it will be more difficult. You also will bounce back into your life, but the memories will remain vivid, reminding you of the ways your life is changing. And it all churns up questions for you to sort out."

Jeff was quiet. Mac sat looking out the window, giving him time. Finally, Jeff spoke. "You're right. My mind and feelings are a mass of contradictions. There are things I need cleared up." Despite the joy Jeff felt after his encounter with Earth, all the old anger and resentment resulting from his experiences with Tami Graves coiled inside of him like a venomous snake primed to attack. "I have to ask bluntly," he blurted, turning to glare at the Synon. "Did your kind do something to me?"

Mac looked pained. "Jeff, we don't 'do things' to anybody. It's against our very nature. For the many years he's known you, Lew Henderson has been aware that you're unique. He sensed your abilities but was reluctant to take steps to verify them, until recent events revealed the extent of your uniqueness."

Thinking of his old friend, Lew, was like a soothing balm to Jeff. He looked a bit sheepish. "It's just a bit much to process."

Mac allowed another moment of silence, then spoke, with a wry smile. "Jeff, your rational mind is fighting to protect you. Logical thought and action have been primary drivers of human survival and adaptation. However, human progress owes much to creativity, vision, and intuition. There's always been a struggle between those impulses. It's imperative that you learn to trust those later ones."

"I know. Since my experience, I've had a sense of euphoria and renewed purpose. All of a sudden, these old resentments resurfaced. Frankly, since meeting Tami, I've felt manipulated, and the resentment festered. I really want to reclaim the feelings I had during and after my encounter with Earth. I'm just beset with seesaw emotions."

"That's natural. You should acknowledge all your reactions and examine their origins, recognizing how human coping and adjustment processes work. You must resist negativity. You must strive to remain positive. It won't always be easy. If you can regain and maintain the state of mind you were in during and after the encounter, you'll be able to achieve your full potential. You can be a great asset to Earth and the life she supports, not the least of which is your own species."

"I just wish these resentments wouldn't suddenly roar to life."

"They will, but the more you concentrate on your work, your loved ones, your partners, and your mission, the sooner they'll fade away. Don't ever hesitate to talk in confidence to me, Lew, or Tami. We've been dealing with people far longer than you have."

Jeff nodded, a slight smile appearing. "Thank you. I realize how fortunate I am. I'll work on myself. I really am enthusiastic about what we might be able to accomplish." A sly grin crept across his face. "So, what about this summer camp? Does it really exist?"

Mac met Jeff's smile with his own. "Not yet. Meeting Emma germinated the idea. She's the first of what we hope will be many. As soon as they become aware of their uniqueness, which can be at any age, of course, it will be difficult for them to maintain life as usual. They will feel different, possibly frightened by their abilities. They will need a safe environment in which to develop—and if they are to aid us, they must develop and be guided, if only for a few months a year."

"So where are you planning to establish this camp?"

"I already own what was previously a summer camp. The compound adjacent to the old farmhouse Lew and I, and now the visiting Synons, live in."

"That place where the rest of the Tech team has little cabins? That was a camp?"

"Of course. It needs some updating and additions but otherwise it's perfect."

"So you plan to wrangle a way to bring Emma into our mission?"

"She's vital. I thought the summer camp would be an effective way to accomplish it. The hurdle will be her parents. I'm afraid they won't be the first reluctant guardians we'll have to deal with, and we need every unique person we can locate. We'll also have to bring your team in on it right away. We need their help."

"Does that mean I'll be able to share what I am with Marie?"

"We've felt that she could best support you by not knowing, but now, we must include her and the team. I need to confer with Lew and Tami."

"Will I be allowed to tell her?"

"I'm sure Lew and Tami will agree that we three Synons should do that." He smiled. "Jeff, my guess is that we'll just be confirming what she already knows. Look back at your connection with Tami when she was in the server fighting Bandela. In her own way, Marie was just as connected to you during that experience. She knew what was happening. And." His smile grew broader. "That night when you met Cosmos. Did Marie blink an eye? She knows you better than any person. Trust her and the bond you share."

Jeff nodded. "The air needs clearing. The secrecy has put a strain on that bond. I insist on being the one to tell her. Alone."

"I still need to confer with the others first, especially the Synon queen, Tami. Please give us the rest of the weekend."

■　■　■

On Monday morning Gary Goodsen released his statement to the press. Its cryptic wording generated a barrage of conspiracy theories across social media, the Web, mainstream and alternative media.

Vera Schechner called Mac on his secure line. "Is this kidnap story why you asked me for Suki's number?" she demanded.

"Isn't it wonderful that the child was found unharmed?" he replied innocently.

"I want to know how Suki is involved. This wording reeks of government cover-up." She plowed right on, ignoring his deflective question.

"Yes it certainly does," he concurred. "Probably an alphabet soup of agencies involved."

"And you weren't right in the pot of soup?"

"Vera, you give me too much power. I work in a small, classified corner. Joint government and local police agencies often form task forces to tackle problems of shared interest. This looks to me like one of those cases. If it's ongoing, then obviously details can't be released. As I said, I'm just relieved the child is safe."

"And what about Suki?"

"I ensured that she's safe."

"I need more."

"Trust that both Suki and Emma Goodsen are safe. I do hope the media doesn't swarm the child's home and those around her. They need peace and quiet."

"Is that a warning?"

"No, just a suggestion. You are a leader and can set the example."

"All right, I'll accept that Suki is okay. So, did anything come of the investigation into Singleton?"

"No. I understand he had a big charity shindig. Hired a lot of security for it. I'll keep digging into him, though, especially his patents and any government contracts. I doubt that will turn up anything I can give you, though."

"I don't have to publicize everything I learn. I'm curious about him. I'll understand if what you find has to remain confidential. I am a patriot, you know."

"I know that very well, Vera. And a person of integrity. Thanks for the tips on him. By the way, did Suki get anything of interest on the UFO stuff? My guy met with her but it seems like they didn't get very far. Gave him some field experience anyway."

"She didn't get much of anything. That's why I'm perplexed about why she might be in danger. There are a bunch of people down there, like lots of places, who are quick to yell UFO at the slightest provocation, but there were no clandestine groups using that as a shield for ulterior motives that she could find. It was a waste of time and money."

"Time to move on, Vera. A lot is still going on with the environment. Looks like melting glaciers and Arctic and Antarctic ice are near the tipping point. I don't think people realize how vulnerable to sea rise coastal areas are. When I think of all the major world cities at risk, I can't understand why people aren't alarmed."

"Heads in sand. You're right. That's an angle to hammer away at. Okay, my friend. Keep me in the loop. Bye for now."

"Good-bye, Vera. You take care."

Vera disconnected and sat in thought. She was grateful that he had taken steps to protect Suki. It spoke of concern beyond the practical. He was simply a good man. *How is it we never have connected on a personal level?* she asked herself. *I'm divorced. Never heard him speak of a wife or significant other. We've been close friends for so long.* She stood up. *Well,* she reminded herself. *People like us are loners, married to our jobs.* Yet a bittersweet mood lingered.

■　■　■

Singleton was apoplectic. The reporter who had called herself Kim Sawa couldn't be located. She didn't appear to have returned to her apartment from the airport. The power was shut off. His people had located nothing about Sawa, Naples, or her work. No address books or material pointing to family or friends were found. They could locate them, of course. Singleton had told his people not to bother, since they would know nothing and questioning them could bring unwanted attention. Bitterness overtook him. He had squandered all his chances to become part of the aliens' inner human circle. He tried to think positively. He might still hear from them again. This lone ship would need to report back to someone for instructions. He just needed to be patient.

*   *   *

Saturday evening, Marie understood that Jeff was so exhausted that he didn't feel like talking. After a quiet dinner, he was on the verge of drifting off, and she sent him to bed. He slept more peacefully and deeply than he had in a long time.

On Sunday morning, Mac called. Jeff wandered down toward the creek with his phone, while Marie sat on the porch with her mug of coffee.

In his usual manner, Mac jumped right into the message. "I conferred with Tami and Lew. We think it's fine for you to tell Marie that recent events and experiences prompted a telepathic ability within you to surface—a trait we think many humans might also have in a latent form. Feel free to tell her about Cosmos if you like. But no other details. Say that more will be explained to her before the upcoming meeting with everyone."

Jeff thanked him, and they hung up. As he slowly walked back to the porch, he unsuccessfully tried to formulate the words he needed. He returned to his rocker and took a sip of coffee. Cosmos jumped into his lap, rubbing his face against Jeff's. "Hi, buddy." Jeff cradled the purring cat.

Marie smiled. "You two have quite the bond." She reached over and stroked the black head.

"We all three have quite the bond," Jeff said, beaming his own smile at her. "Marie, I'm really sorry I wasn't allowed to be honest with you. All that's about to change." Her eyebrows rose.

She set down her mug and peered at him. He just let the words tumble out. "I think you've known since all this began that I'm a bit…different…from most people."

"Uh-huh." She nodded.

He rushed on. "The Synons think many people are actually like me." She nodded again, maintaining eye contact. "I seem to be telepathic."

She laughed. "What a look on your face! You don't have to be scared to say that. I've suspected it, and more. I mean, didn't Cosmos tell you Tami had sent him?" Her eyebrows rose again.

Jeff emitted a loud sigh. "What a relief. Marie, you're gonna be so blown away by what's happened recently. Mac said not to tell you. They'll explain it all very soon." He picked up his mug, noticing it was empty. "Is there more coffee?"

*   *   *

Lana Adams and Mannie Patel wore the same stunned expression, then looked at each other and started whooping and dancing in their chairs. Marie smiled wanly. Jeff sat looking down at his hands folded on the table, his face slightly flushed.

Chris was the first to find his voice. "I was there! Well, not with Jeff and Emma when they spoke with…her. But I joined everyone when they returned to Tami's room. I can't believe what's happened these past few days!" His eyes seemed about to pop out of his head.

Lew was beaming. "The Living World surely led us to this team."

Marie had sat silently, her gaze roving among those who sat around the table with her. She looked near tears. Tami said gently, "Marie, we apologize. In order to cushion the shock, we needed all of you to learn these astounding things in the carefully chosen words you just heard."

Marie managed a half smile. "Thank you. In retrospect, the fact that Jeff achieved this accomplishment is not really shocking to me. I am sad that he was prevented from sharing it with me privately." The pained look she gave Jeff broke his heart.

Now, it was Tami who appeared to be near tears. When she spoke her voice was barely audible. "We made a mistake."

After a few moments of silence in which no eyes around the table met, Jeff cleared his throat. "I appreciate you admitting that, Tami. In truth, I'm still trying to articulate it in my mind. I'm not sure I could have adequately related it to anyone. It was the most astounding experience of my life." He grinned. "I did share it with Cosmos. He wasn't at all surprised but was proud of me."

That broke the mood. Laughter rang out around the table. Lew drawled, "I think we should officially make Cosmos a team member."

Mac had been uncharacteristically quiet. Now, his commanding voice filled the room. "Lew is right that The Living World brought us all together. With Emma and our many earth-dwelling Synon friends, we are about to embark on a mission that could span the globe." He looked at each of the five humans and five Synons. "We are just getting started."

■　■　■

EPILOGUE

In the Realm, there had been a sense of foreboding brought on by Earth's anguish. Learning of Jeff and Emma's communication with her gave the Synons renewed hope. Under Tork's guidance, they concluded that all efforts should be put into the plans for marshalling the knowledge and experience of earth-dwelling Synons to expedite the search for "unique" humans, as they had come to call them, in hopes of soothing Earth's turbulence and persuading her human population to work together to mitigate climate change.

Tork returned to the Tech Center bearing the affirmation of the Realm for their plan. A small portion of his vast awareness had maintained a strand of connection with Emma. He had been flabbergasted by the telepathic exchanges between her and Jeff. Earth's effusive reaction to them was the most positive event so far. It seemed Earth had provided them with the remedy for her illness. It was time to move ahead with implementing their plans. He and Tami were thrilled with Mac's ideas for a summer camp. They recognized the immense task ahead of not only locating "uniques," but of convincing them that their abilities could literally save the planet. Tangles of logistics loomed. It would take the enormous intellectual power of many Synons and a few unique humans to accomplish this new mission.

. . .

TuMa'Aye Gra'vay now recognized that through her experiences as Tami Graves she had developed the capacity to truly empathize with humans by embodying, rather than impersonating, their thoughts and feelings. She now felt an intrinsic bond with humans more powerful than ever in her long existence. It would prove invaluable in the work ahead.

Their plan was already in progress. Earth had responded to Jeff and Emma in a way she never had with any Synons. Most extraordinary was Emma's instant comprehension of Earth's message. Only humans like her and Jeff could help Earth battle her own immune responses to people's destructiveness.

When she and the group of Synons had convened with Earth at the mountain river, each Synon was impressed with the face of a specific human. Those Synons had dispersed to search them out. It seemed plausible that each face might belong to a person who could be found in close proximity to where that specific Synon lived, so that was where each started. Uniques would not only be found in the Appalachians where these Synon personas resided, but it was a good beginning.

. . .

Look for **Convergence: The Living World Book Three**
later in 2022.

ACKNOWLEDGMENTS

My sincere gratitude goes to everyone who has purchased and read ***Passageways: The Living World Book One***. Your support, comments, and reviews have encouraged me in the completion of ***Precarious*** and in planning the third installment of this series, ***Convergence***, which you can look forward to later in 2022.

I'm grateful to all those who have helped and encouraged me in the development of this series: family; friends; my colleagues/friends in Write On! Writers; and others who have encouraged and advised me, especially in the North Carolina Writers Network. I gleaned valuable information from the Alliance of Independent Authors.

Special appreciation goes to Susan Snowden for editorial assistance and Michelle Owen, book and cover design. I've received many comments on the beautiful and creative look of ***Passageways*** and know that the design of ***Precarious*** will be equally as well received.

You might notice that the cover image for ***Precarious*** is similar to that of ***Passageways***. It is a detail from the same stunning assemblage of 48 frames taken with Hubble Space Telescope's Advanced Camera for Surveys of the Carina Nebula, NGC3372, which is within our own Milky Way Galaxy, 7,500 light years away. It shows stars in the process of formation. You'll see another amazing detail in the third installment of ***The Living World.***

Please look at https://esahubble.org/ for more information and to view breathtaking images from the Hubble Space Telescope. As one of humankind's major innovations, this space-based observatory provides unprecedented knowledge and research opportunities. A collaboration between ESA (European Space Agency) and NASA, it's an example of what international cooperation can accomplish.

AFTERWORD

Writing fiction, even of the speculative form, requires much more research and verification than would be expected. I have tried to render depictions of named places, organizations, and practices as accurately as possible within my fictional framework, and I apologize for any misconceptions. As with **Passageways**, I've taken "poetic liberty" to invent specific locations in named places for the sake of my plot.

Popular culture and entertainment references are made in a spirit of tribute.

The scientific references are based on real and theoretically postulated principles and practices. If they tweak your interest, please research to learn more about them. Of course, the fun of writing speculative fiction is that an author can move far beyond proven fact, like personifying our planet Earth, as has been done in various ways for millennia. In this fictional mythology she is but one link in an interconnected, interdimensional construct—The Living World.

Please follow me on:

My Amazon Author page: **https://www.amazon.com/author/ patriciavestal-livingworld-bks**

My Facebook Author Page where you can comment and ask questions: **https://www.facebook.com/pvestalauthor**

For my blog and more information visit **www.seaofmountains press.com**

I appreciate reviews posted on the sites where you purchase my books. They help me to shape the next book. Please consider asking your local independent bookstore to stock the series, especially if you live in an area in which scenes of the books take place.

Again, thanks to all who read this series. It's meant as entertaining speculative fiction, but I hope it prompts everyone who reads it to a renewed appreciation of Nature and to do whatever seems appropriate and feasible to help our unique Earth and the life she nourishes.

ABOUT THE AUTHOR

After working in publishing and higher education in New York and Florida, Patricia Vestal has returned to her native North Carolina's mountains where she writes and conducts writing courses. Patricia's publications include her first novel ***Passageways: The Living World Book One***, short fiction, reviews, and essays. Her plays have had readings and stage and television productions. She's a member of the North Carolina Writers Network, the Dramatists Guild, and the Alliance of Independent Authors. She earned her Communications BA from State University of New York and an MA in Drama from New York University. Follow her at www.seaofmountainspress.com and **https://www.facebook.com/pvestalauthor**.

ABOUT PRECARIOUS

Embark on a kaleidoscope of adventure with young Cherokee IT tech Jeff Hawke as he's swept into a maelstrom linking a kidnapping, a wealthy entrepreneur seeking to aid extraterrestrials, Earth's reaction to human disregard, and Synons. These shapeshifting energy-spirit-mind beings are from the Realm, a universe tethered to Earth by Passageways through which they travel to nourish and maintain the symbiotic bond with Earth and her inhabitants to The Living World. The Synons enlist Jeff's help in attempts to relieve Earth's increasing distress, which is threatening to destroy her and all those she supports.

Like **Passageways: The Living World Book One**, you'll find **Precarious** immersing you in the adventures and conflicts experienced by Jeff Hawke along with familiar and new characters. Just when Jeff is settling into his rustic home near the government tech center hidden in North Carolina's mountains where he now works, his mission leads to danger and startling revelations. Can he and his allies discover the answer to saving Earth?